PRAISE FOR P.D. SINGER

Fire on the Mountain —Rainbow Awards Jury's Choice Honorable Mention

"This was a well written, engrossing story and I can't wait to see where this series goes from here."
    —Pants Off Reviews

"…a sexy and fun and sweet story."
    —Under the Covers

Snow on the Mountain

"I highly recommend *Snow on the Mountain* to anyone who likes a romance mixed with misunderstanding, scandal, adventure, a little possessiveness, and a secret cabin in the mountains. It is as fun as it is sweet."
    —Joyfully Jay

"…another treat from Ms. Singer and I really enjoyed it."
    —Mrs. Condit Reads

Blood on the Mountain — Rainbow Awards Finalist, Honorable Mention (5*)

Read it for a cracking plot, and a wonderful couple that deserve their Happy Ever After.
    —Mrs. Condit Reads

Fall Down the Mountain

P.D. SINGER

ROCKY RIDGE BOOKS

Fall Down the Mountain
Copyright © 2020 by P.D. Singer
Cover Art by Cosmic Letterz

Print ISBN: 978-1-62622-086-7

First edition Torquere Press 2010
Second edition Dreamspinner Press 2012

Published 2020 3rd Edition

Rocky Ridge Books
Box 6922
Broomfield, CO 80021

ALSO BY P.D. SINGER

The Mountains series (Novels/Novellas)

Into the Mountains (Kurt and Jake)

Snow on the Mountain (Kurt and Jake)

Fall Down the Mountain (Mark and Allan)

Blood on the Mountain (Kurt and Jake)

Return to the Mountain (Gary and Seth)

Coming Out from the Mountain (Kurt and Jake)

Novels

Running to Him (Men of Monument Book 1)

The Rare Event

A New Man

Diving Deep

Spokes

Concierge Service

For everyone who said, "You can't leave Mark like that!"

Fall Down the MOUNTAIN

PROLOGUE

The snow beneath my skis shattered. Cracks opened below me —the solid snowpack disintegrated and slid. Snow would crash down the mountain, carrying away anything, everything in its path. Unimaginable tons would roar down the chute where two peaks met. Only the bedrock of the mountains could withstand the avalanche. Nothing on the surface would defy it, certainly not puny specks of humans.

I hurtled toward the two skiers, bellowing, "Get off the slab! Get off the slab!" They weren't moving fast enough. My training screamed *Get away! Leave them both!* My heart said *No!* but I could only save one. Acting before I could think, I swooped to the side, catching one man. He stayed on his feet, else I'd have to leave him. Or die with him, if we didn't reach the trees.

My survival vest would inflate into a big red ruff. I might live if the slide caught us. He wouldn't. It would keep me at the surface. Him, too, for a few seconds. The roaring maelstrom would tear us apart.

The mountain detonated before we reached the trees. White

1

spume hid the sky; the snowpack exploded in a deadly bellow. The hill fell apart beneath us.

We fought to reach higher ground. I lost my grip—the snow stole him from my hand. He screamed, tumbling downhill. The pounding of the avalanche drowned any words. I could only watch helplessly from the trees, yelling, "Take my hand!" My outstretched arm wasn't long enough. Fifteen arms wouldn't be long enough. The chaos swallowed him.

Did it last a minute? An hour? I couldn't tear my eyes from where he had been. The horror—eternal—I'd see his panicked face forever.

The mountain quieted. I sped to the faraway hillock in the snow, horribly certain of what I'd find. Like a compass needle to north, I skied straight to that mound, tearing the shovel off my belt. "Be alive!" I begged, throwing scoops of snow behind me. "Be alive!"

The snow, hard as concrete, came away in clumps as I dug. Finally, blond hair and a red jacket appeared—I dug faster and could finally brush the snow from his face. "Breathe!" I commanded. "I'll get you out!"

His eyes were open, but he was still. Too still. No breath. No movement. Kurt looked up sightlessly from the snow. I hadn't saved him after all.

"No!" I screamed to the uncaring mountain that threw my words back to me:"Nooooooo!"

ONE

I woke up screaming, my heart thudding painfully in my chest. It took me a few minutes to breathe normally again. Unfortunately, I probably also woke up everyone else on the other side of the paper-thin walls. Wapiti Creek might be sensible about providing shelter to the resort employees in these three story apartment buildings on the edge of town, but they hadn't spent the money to make them as sturdy or soundproof as the million-dollar condos or fancy hotels.

"Shut up, McAvoy!" My neighbor usually called me Mark. A month and a half of sharing my nightmares had reduced him to last names and pounding the walls.

I wasn't screaming because I wanted to, damn it! I didn't wake like this two or three times a week because I enjoyed it! The avalanche was real, but not the way I dreamed it this time. Someone died in the snow but not Kurt, the ski instructor whose face I saw tonight. No, Kurt had fled down the black diamond chute. Jake and I truly reached the trees and held each other tightly while the mountain went berserk. We survived, clutching each other in the illusion that my one avalanche vest would keep us both at the surface. The snow would have ripped us apart, but we held each other all the same.

The one who died was Ulf, and I couldn't really argue that the world was worse off for his loss. Ulf had been shooting at Kurt, who escaped before the slide started. Jake knocked him down before he could kill anyone, and then I swooped in to drag Jake off the slab. Ulf had had to look out for himself.

It was Ulf's face that we finally revealed in the snow, staring and sightless, frozen and broken. It took Marty, the other patrollers, and me hours to find where he was buried. Hours that gave him time to suffocate in his own carbon dioxide exhalations, time to lose all body function from the severed nerves in his spine. The avalanche snapped him like a twig—even if we'd found him fast, he would never have survived being loaded on the stretcher. I saw him again in my sleep, white-faced and still, more often than I cared to think about, but he didn't make me scream in the night.

No, the screaming nights happened when I got Jake or Kurt mixed up in the dreams. There were nights where the rescue that really happened got muddled with the real death, nights where it didn't work out that Jake and I were still standing when the snow stopped moving. He and I got far enough up the side of the slope that the avalanche missed us, and we hadn't known until later that Kurt made it out okay.

Jake kissed me for joy when the snow settled back to the ground and the sky turned blue again. I kissed him out of joy and for wanting in those moments, knowing it was all I'd ever get. He brushed the snow off my face and kissed me, glad to be alive, and if he hadn't immediately thought of Kurt, he might have kissed me some more. I wanted those kisses; I wanted a chance with him, a chance that wouldn't come. Since the avalanche, it was crystal clear I had no chance with Jake.

I screamed every night I dug Jake out of the snow.

I screamed louder on nights I dug up Kurt. It wasn't just the horror of his death, it was hatred of myself. The nights Kurt died, I asked myself if I hadn't tried hard enough, if I dug too slowly. If I let him die. For a chance with a man who would always wonder if I hadn't tried hard enough. For a chance that wouldn't exist.

The nights Ulf died were almost good nights by comparison.

I sat bolt upright on awakening, with my heart thudding against my ribs. The dream was especially vivid this time. Every strand of blond hair showed clearly against Kurt's pale forehead; little balls of snow clung to lashes that didn't blink them away. I couldn't shake the feeling that death had visited for real tonight —lying back down wasn't going to happen. I tried, but the bedding was clammy and the sense of doom too strong. Pulling on a pair of flannel pants, I thought I'd go sit on my big easy chair in the living room, but my feet took me farther.

The building was quiet at two a.m., the hall lights almost too bright. I padded the length of the third floor to the central stairs. One flight down and then about halfway across the other wing of the building brought me to a door I had passed through before, bringing Jake home.

He'd been drunk and upset; I suggested taking him upstairs until he sobered up. He went home instead, to a Kurt who was angry and upset for reasons that came out only after Kurt and I smacked each other around awhile. I got a black eye to commemorate our better understanding. I might get another one tonight.

Because I had to knock on that door. I needed to see for myself that the men who lived on the other side were alive and well, and then I might be able to sleep again. If not tonight, then some other night, but the need to see them both, to touch them and feel the warmth of life, pulled my hand up to the wood. I knocked.

Three soft raps on the door, and only then did I realize I had no idea what to say, how to explain being on their doorstep in the wee hours.

The door opened and Kurt stood before me, puzzled and knuckling one eye. "Hey, Mark. What's the matter?" He opened the door wide enough to let me into the dimly lit living room. He wore a T-shirt and soft pants, and his blond hair was tousled from sleep, or maybe from having Jake's hands in it. I didn't want to think about that.

"I...." I didn't have any words yet. Maybe my haggard expression said something. "I needed...." I needed to get out of there. Jake was coming around the corner, pulling down a T-shirt he probably hadn't been wearing a few minutes ago. His flannel pants hung around his hips at a dangerously low level, more suited for a jockey than a six-foot-tall hunk. His brown hair stuck up on one side from the pillow; his wide brown eyes grew more alert and filled with concern with each second I stood stammering.

"Mark, are you okay?" He exchanged a quick glance with Kurt before focusing on me again.

I shook my head wordlessly. I wasn't okay, but I didn't know how to say it, and now that I was here with two handsome, warm, live men, I felt unbelievably stupid that I'd let a nightmare chase me down the hall to them.

"Hey, you're with friends," Jake said, placing his hand on my upper arm. His touch burned. I'd spent a lot of hours imagining his hands on me, and now he was touching me, in front of his lover. I knew they were lovers—Jake had told me right off that he wasn't available, but he left the door open for friendship. I never needed friends as badly as I needed them now.

"Yeah." I didn't move, but Kurt came a step closer and took my other arm.

"Crappy night?" he asked.

I nodded, not trusting myself to speak. I looked at him straight on, seeing finely modeled features and blue eyes framed by wavy blond hair, and nothing but concern.

"We've had one or two of those. And our reasons aren't as good as yours." Kurt, Jake, and Marty—who was downstairs snuggled up to Chelsea, no doubt—were the only ones who knew what really happened the day of the avalanche. The official story didn't tell the half of it. "How can we help?"

"Just...." I lifted a hand to his face. Somehow, I knew that if I touched Kurt, rather than Jake, it would be okay, that he'd understand it was warmth and life I needed. I stroked his face, feeling the stubble on his skin, tracing his features, letting my fingers follow the curve of his cheek. He allowed it, saying nothing as I trailed my fingers down his neck and then placed my hand flat just below his breastbone. "Just keep breathing, okay?"

He nodded and took a large breath, letting me feel the rise and fall in his chest, never taking his eyes from my face. "I will." Kurt breathed for me, and Jake let him, his hand still on my arm. The cold lump in my belly thawed a tiny bit with every movement in Kurt's chest, proving my fear tonight was only a nightmare. "Did I stop for a while?" he asked after a time.

"Yeah. Some nights it's Jake." I closed my eyes, trying to chase those memories back, but Jake had a better way to do it. He took my other hand and placed it on his chest, letting me feel the ribs and muscles pull the air in and push it out of him.

"Had a few of those nights myself. Kurt wakes me." Jake

hadn't taken his hand from mine; he pressed it more tightly against his body with each breath.

I wished someone would be there to wake me before I got to the screaming stage. There was no one to share my bed or my life—the only one I'd been interested in had his hand over mine right now. I'd been in a lot of beds, but not with anyone who cared enough to wake me unless I disturbed him. Sleeping alone was better than that, but the sheer barrenness of my life put a catch in my throat.

Jake misinterpreted it. "Mark, have you ever mourned Ulf?"

"Not sure why I would—he was no friend of mine." Ulf had no friends I knew of. "Just keep breathing." I spoke both to them and to me, because my chest had gotten tight.

"He sure was no friend of ours either, but he died, and we were there and involved. My nightmares didn't stop until I thought about that for a while." Jake pressed my hand against his chest a little harder. Kurt breathed more deeply.

I wouldn't grieve, but I could think. "He died because he was stupid, greedy, and mean. He died because he was trying to kill people. Kill you. I know he was shooting. The mountain would have hidden the body for him—we might have not known to look." I swayed a little, trying not to yell into the quiet night. "He died, and we didn't. Except we all nearly did. Because of him."

"But we didn't," Jake pointed out. "Because of you."

"Do you remember what Marty said the day it all happened?" Kurt asked quietly. "I do."

"That I saved the right people?" I asked bitterly. Wrapping my arms around myself might have kept me from shivering.

"Yeah." Kurt didn't release my hand. "You did."

"I did, but it wasn't enough." There was a lump the size of a mountain in my throat now; the words came out in a whisper.

"You would have saved us all if you could." Jake gathered me against his chest, wrapped me in those strong arms. "I know you would have." He pressed my head against his shoulder. "Even Ulf."

"Even him," Kurt said from behind me, where he'd come very close. Close enough to press against me, to hold me from behind with his own strong arms.

Together they held me and let me cry at last for the man I couldn't save.

TWO

It may have taken a while to cry myself out, and it left me feeling strangely light, floaty. Exhausted. From the safety of their arms I could grieve, some for Ulf, some for me. I'd done all that I could, and it wasn't enough. The tears washed away something and its absence might let me sleep again.

The warmth at my back left and then Kurt returned with a wet washcloth and a handful of tissues. Jake didn't let me go while Kurt cleaned my face and let me blow my nose, just patted me gently as I subsided into hiccups. "Do you need to hit the bathroom first?" he asked.

Huh? "No."

"Then give us a sec." Kurt slipped his arm back around me, mystifying me, and then he explained all. "You shouldn't be alone tonight." He started walking me toward the back of the apartment, and Jake made it clear he agreed when he steered me along with a hand on my shoulder.

This was both everything I wanted and everything I didn't. Not being alone. Being in bed with Jake, whose warm brown eyes told me I was welcome when I looked back at him for clues. Being in bed with Kurt, whose boyfriend I'd spent a lot of time fantasizing about. But most of all, not being alone.

The center of the bed was still warm when they parked me. I told myself I should escape while they were in the bathroom, brushing teeth or whatever they'd do in there, but I couldn't force myself out of the bed. Slinking away while their backs were turned was not just dishonorable but stupid, given that I couldn't expect to be invited back. While I debated, I heard, "He's...." and then the sound of running water covered up their plotting. I should get out of here before I meddled in the relationship. I'd already disrupted their night's sleep and didn't want more serious crimes laid on me. But before I could slide out of bed, they were padding back and slipping in beside me, one on each side.

"It's okay, Mark, you're here because both of us think you should be." Jake pulled me back against his side. "We'll wake you if you dream again." He still had the flannel pants on but had discarded the sodden T-shirt. My head fit unexpectedly well against his bare shoulder, though my feet stuck off the end of the bed, since I was actually about an inch taller than him.

"Uh..." was the best thing I could come up with, and Kurt laughed softly. He snuggled up against my back.

"No one's wished you sweet dreams, and you haven't gotten them." Kurt pressed the side of his face against the back of my head, and then had to stroke my hair down to pin it with his cheek. It's longish and fine and probably flew up in a staticky brown cloud into his nose. "So, sweet dreams."

"Yeah, sweet dreams." Jake nuzzled my forehead. They put their arms over me, clasping each other's upper arms to be my barrier against the night.

Even in my exhaustion, I didn't think I could ignore the hottest two friends I'd ever had pressed up against me. Kurt was being damned understanding about me throwing an arm over his lover's naked chest, and Jake hadn't moved Kurt's groin away from my butt. I've been celibate too long, I thought, wondering if I could really fall asleep like this. But before I could organize any protest, I was out.

The dream, when it came, was different. The avalanche took us all this time, and I was buried like the others, crushed by tons of snow. Struggling to breathe, struggling to move, struggling to wake up and out of this, I flailed but was pinned fast. Swimming to consciousness went faster because I could hear soft voices calling my name, feel hands drawing me from the snow.

"Shh, Mark, it's okay, you're okay, we're all okay, you're safe," came from both sides of me, with soft brushes of lips against my head. "We're here, you're safe in bed, you're with us." That didn't make any sense at first, until abruptly it did. I'd probably been feeling their warm weight on either side and mixed it in with the dream. I tensed, angry that what had been a good idea turned out to make my nightmare worse, and then flopped back against them, knowing I'd wakened from more horrible dreams the hard way. Gentle hands stroked my shoulder and side, reminding me softly that I was alive.

The dream faded away under their touch, replaced with an equally uncomfortable awareness. I was alive and safe, held by someone I found incredibly attractive. Also by someone who was extremely attractive if not the object of my interest. Kurt was soothing me, but Jake was doing the opposite. Once again, he was holding me after an avalanche, and though the slide was only in my head this time, my reaction was just as much in my body as before. We'd broken apart then so he could search for Kurt, but Kurt was right there with us now, and the two of them were embracing me.

I tensed again, aware that my cock had hardened and was pressed against Jake's thigh. Last time, I don't think he'd noticed, but now it was about as obvious as my nose, and holding still wasn't going to keep him from figuring it out. I'd have to move.

They let me roll to my back and propped themselves on their elbows so they could look down into my face. The small clock by the bed shed enough light to see their concern, and probably they could see my embarrassment. So I shut my eyes.

"It's okay, Mark. This is why you're here." Jake leaned down and kissed my forehead. That was not where I wanted that kiss. I should get up, right now. Their arms were over my chest, and I couldn't make myself leave them.

Kurt leaned down to nuzzle my hair. "How're you doing?" he murmured.

"I... should go." Telling him the real state of affairs wouldn't do.

"Don't think so," he surprised me by saying. "Mark, we know a little bit about surviving." Jake snorted, a rather full sound for the quiet of the night. Kurt glanced up at him, down toward my feet, and back to my face. "Well, we do."

He did now. Because if he'd been trying to see my feet, they were obscured by the tent in the blanket. Rolling over hadn't hidden a thing.

"Your body needs to be convinced as much as your head does." Kurt put his face down to mine to kiss me full on the mouth. "You aren't going anywhere."

I couldn't have gone anywhere after that without wild horses dragging me. He kissed me again, swallowing my little whimpers, because in a minute, Jake was going to kiss me, and his hand had already started a slow path up and down my chest.

We let our lips part slightly, and he finished the kiss with little nibbles on my lower lip.

"Wait…" I finally got out, and they both said "Yes?"

"Let me…" I rose up and tried to slide my hands under them. They lifted away from the mattress enough to let me do it, and then I lay flat, my arms pinned. I was being offered more than I could imagine, by men who were so clearly a couple that there had to be a way to tell them I wouldn't beg for more than they wanted to give. Effectively immobilizing myself should do it; everything from now on would be their choice. I could touch about a six inch arc on their backs, but they could have anything they wanted with me.

Kurt took his mouth from mine. He'd kissed me, knowing how I felt about Jake, telling me it was all right to take the caress his lover was bringing down to me. Jake kissed me softly at first, but the intensity grew, our lips parting, our tongues meeting, and Kurt rested his hand on my belly. Having my arms stuck beneath them was the only thing keeping me from rolling on top of Jake and trying to plunder his mouth. As it was, he kissed me pretty damned thoroughly.

I would have kept exploring him, but he lifted away from me and turned to Kurt, who had already gotten more than kisses tonight, I'd bet. Their faces turned at an angle, letting their lips meet over me, and then Kurt came back down to me, followed by Jake.

Having a "generous" mouth was a good thing for the first time in my entire life. I've always been self-conscious about how wide my mouth is, but now it meant I had enough kiss for both of them at once. Their hands left me and slipped over one another as they covered me, and all I could do was stroke the small swaths of skin I could reach on their backs. I didn't try to reach under Kurt's T-shirt, but Jake's skin was smooth and hot against mine.

People would start rapping on walls if I didn't tone down the sound effects, so I tried to keep the moaning low, but oh it was good. They'd gone back to kisses for me, then kisses for each other, and they caressed me again. Each of them had a hand under my T-shirt, finding a nipple now and then, always moving. I was moving, too, because my good intentions about not reaching for too much couldn't keep my hips still.

My cock was throbbing hard and leaking, my balls were drawn up tight against my body, and I thrust upward to the blankets that still covered us. They hadn't reached into my flannel sleep pants yet, only down to the waistband, and the wait was sweet torment. If they didn't reach, it would be a torment I'd have to take care of alone, but then Jake and Kurt exchanged some sort of wordless communication. Little nods before more kisses, and one of them untied the drawstring.

I did cry out now, with one hand rubbing down my thigh, gripping the inside while the other went flat against my belly, following the treasure trail to my base. They played with my body beneath the flannel for a long delicious time, touching my belly, thighs, and hips but not my cock. I bucked against them and mouthed any part that came into range. I had my face against Jake's shoulder when they got down to business at last, and I didn't try to sort out the hands that cupped my balls, rolling them under the skin, and gripped my hard shaft to pump me. I was wound too tight; it had been too long and the need was too great now for me to make it last, though they weren't in any hurry. Kurt pressed his lips against my ear as I cried out against Jake's arm. Vaguely I thought Jake might have been kissing Kurt's head, but it didn't matter—strong hands stroked me in the way only another man could. Two hands now around my cock, both of them gripped me. I thrust against them, their own hips pressed against mine but not pinning me down. I held them close and they held me closer; the orgasm ripped through me, pulsing and spurting as I set my teeth into Jake's flesh.

Shuddering with the last ripples of my climax, I collapsed against the mattress. A small, thin sound escaped as I held onto the last of the orgasm, which made them chuckle. "Quite sure you're alive now?" Jake asked, and he did kiss me again before looking to see how much damage I'd done to his biceps. I was a little embarrassed about that—should have warned him I was a biter.

"Either I'm one hundred percent alive or I just died happy," I mumbled, and Kurt laughed aloud, letting go of me and slipping his hand out of my pants.

"Stay right there," he suggested, and he was back in a moment with a washcloth. Jake let go of me, and that made me moan for another reason. This was the only bit of paradise I'd get with him, and I didn't want it to be over. I'd do whatever he and Kurt wanted for their own pleasure, but neither was making suggestions, except that I should roll to my side against Kurt's back.

"Snuggle up," Jake murmured into my ear as he curled up against my back, nearly undoing my resolve not to push back against him. Kurt tucked himself against my front, making me the center spoon. "You'll sleep well now, and you'll be fine." He brushed his lips against the back of my neck, and Kurt stroked the arm I tossed around him.

I told myself not to be disappointed that it was ending now, when I couldn't have hoped there would be even this much. The wishing kept me awake about another two minutes before the post-orgasmic lassitude and sheer exhaustion pulled me under, and this time nothing woke me until the sun came through the window.

I tried to get out of bed without disturbing the guys, but Kurt woke anyway. He quietly watched me stroke Jake's hair and admire his strong, handsome features, and then Kurt walked me to the door.

"Thanks," I started, before sputtering to a stop. "I…."

"It's okay," he said, one hand on the doorknob and the other on my arm. "You needed it."

"Still…" I started again. "I know it was a one-time thing. And I won't try to make it into anything else. But thanks."

"It's what friends do. Once." He smiled with one side of his mouth, but it did reach his eyes.

"Not every friend." Not any that I'd ever had. "Why?"

"Because." And he looked off into some distance before bringing his eyes back to me. "I don't want to say because we owed you one, though we do. You kept Jake alive that day, and I've never thanked you for it."

No, they didn't owe me a thing. Jake had thanked me with his tongue down my throat and that had to be enough. I tried to keep that off my face, though not successfully, I guess.

"You're looking guilty now," he chided me gently. "Surviving an avalanche is extenuating circumstances. It did happen and he was there, and it's okay."

The air went out of me in a rush. "How did you…?"

"He told me, Mark. The same day. Won't say I was thrilled, but I also said we know something about surviving disasters. You both were glad to be alive." He gripped my shoulder. "I'm glad we're all three alive."

"If it's not owing," I said slowly, trying to digest this revelation, "then what?"

He paused a long while, making me sorry I asked. Before I

could say, "You don't have to tell me," he went on haltingly. "It's, well, Jake and I both like you. You're a friend and an honorable man. We trust you. And—" He took a deep breath. "Jake's never been with anyone except me. And I want to keep it that way, but I also don't want him to look around in ten years, wondering what he'd missed, and think he has to go find it."

"I see." I did, really. I was there, in need, trustworthy, and safe because he was there. Maybe I wasn't so safe, because I could push it, though I wouldn't. "Kurt, I don't think he's going to be looking at anyone but you in ten years' time. He'd be a fool if he did." I enveloped him in a hug and kissed the bridge of his nose. "Share that with Jake, with interest." A squeeze to his shoulder and then I was out of there.

As I trudged down the hall to the sound of a shutting door, I thought about what I really wanted. It wasn't Jake; he was more out of reach than before he'd wrapped that big hand around my cock. What I really wanted wasn't him—I wanted what he and Kurt had together.

I wished myself luck finding it.

THREE

"Daddy, do you think we're almost ready to go on the black diamond hills?" five-almost-six-and don't forget -that-Daddy-year-old Todd asked his craggy but handsome father, putting his fork down in his empty bowl. "You saw how good we're getting." He kicked his twin sister under the table.

Gracie chimed in. "Yeah, Daddy! We skied all day, and we didn't fall down at all! Mommy did, but she's going faster now. Jake only fell down once, and that's 'cause Todd tripped him." She ate a bite of stew and kicked her brother back. The childish antics seemed out of place in the elegant dining room.

James Underwood chuckled at his offspring, who had been nagging to ski the expert slopes since the season started. They'd begun skiing practically the moment they grew into the smallest equipment available, as befitted the children of the man who owned the mountain. "You'll be ready soon, I think. Did you have a lesson with Kurt today?" He got big smiles and enthusiastic nods from the sprouts, and a less-than-thrilled nod from his lovely young wife, Melanie.

He liked the young men almost as much as his children did,

though for slightly different reasons. Gracie and Todd adored Jake because he would spend some of his day off skiing with them, but they worshipped Kurt because he was teaching them to ski the way their heroes on the US Ski Team did. No less a personage than Jorey Taylor, Olympic medalist and sometime Nerf-soccer player in the Underwood living room, had assured them Kurt could do it. Underwood sincerely hoped so, because his great fear was that the twins would slip their leashes and head down one of those black diamond slopes. Or worse, they might head for a double black diamond slope, thinking it would be twice as much fun, instead of understanding that it was the steepest, most challenging and dangerous terrain on the mountain.

"Maybe we do Dynamite Alley for our birthday?" Gracie wheedled. "We'll be six and much bigger then." Big brown eyes beamed sincerity in her belief that a month would make such a huge difference.

"No promises." A second chance at fatherhood had taught Underwood not to phrase things in any way likely to be misunderstood or twisted by the children. Claire, his first wife and mother of his older children, had been quite good at heading off arguments, though Melanie, sulking across the table from him now, didn't deal with the twins as efficiently. He changed the subject before anyone could protest again. "Dinner was delicious, Mel. Old family recipe?" He knew perfectly well that if it was, it wasn't her family's. He'd been paying more attention to the credit card charges lately.

"No," she admitted. "I called Almost Home again, because I knew I was going to be out on the slopes all afternoon with Kurt." She got something of a sneer into his name. "We worked on turns."

"Good. You need that. Ulf hadn't gotten you into proper

parallel turns." Ulf as a ski instructor left a great deal to be desired, in James Underwood's estimation. "You've improved several levels since changing ski schools." He let that hang in the air for a moment. "Charlie says the students are happy with Kurt. He's certainly an excellent skier. An excellent instructor." He let that hang in the air a moment, too. *Unlike Ulf* might as well have come out of Underwood's mouth. "I did some checking." *As I should have done earlier* also vibrated unsaid.

"May we be excused?" Todd and Gracie asked from behind cleaned dishes. Underwood caught the twins' quick glances toward their mother's face, pale against her long dark hair. Her smudged mauve lipstick looked unnatural next to the sudden whiteness of her skin.

"Yes, you may." Underwood wanted the kids out of earshot for the next matters he'd discuss with Melanie. He glanced at a young woman watching from the doorway, signaling her to collect her young charges.

"And can we do Hotdog Bun for our birthday?" The black diamond hills were never far from the children's minds.

Still no promises, though he did tell them to clear their plates from the table and "Kiss Mama an extra kiss, because we won't be seeing her for a few days."

Melanie froze, but accepted the children's affections without saying anything, though her eyes widened for an instant when Todd moaned, "I thought you weren't going skiing with Ulf again?"

Their father didn't explain other than to say, "No, kids, Ulf doesn't ski here anymore."

The nanny escorted the children away from the table and toward the tub, leaving James Underwood alone with his wife. "No, Ulf doesn't ski here anymore, does he, Melanie?"

She flinched at the question but didn't respond.

"The twins and I have been left alone quite often so you could ski with Ulf. We've seen an unprecedented amount of you since he was killed in the avalanche. You know, Melanie, I don't mind you hiring people to do things." He steepled his fingers and looked over them at her. "A nanny, fine. A housekeeper, fine. Almost Home to make dinner, also fine—Allan cooks much better than you do. A ski instructor, certainly—hire the best. However, I object to you hiring a sex partner. Did you attend the memorial service for Ulf? Or did you have one privately, while wearing the black underwear of mourning?"

She quavered. "It wasn't like that, James!"

"Really?" He didn't roar at her. He'd found it was much more effective to quietly deliver a blow. "What was it, then?"

"He taught me to ski." She stuck out her chin defiantly.

"Apparently not, judging by your progress since Thanksgiving. Melanie, please. Don't take me for a fool. Those attractive young ski bums who scan lift tickets scanned yours every run you made. Wapiti Creek knows exactly what the lift utilization is of every visitor through here—that's one way I make this resort profitable. I know who bought each and every season pass, and how much each gets used. The Alpenschlössl Ski School season tickets show some very unusual patterns. Would you care to guess?" He gave her hard eyes over the maple table.

"Probably a lot of bunny runs. That's what we did." Melanie's full lips, normally attractive, drew into a thin line.

"That too." He had to admire the way she tried to brazen her way through his revelations. "Several bunny runs in the morning, then either nothing or one trip up the Lower Scott lift and another up the Upper Scott to the expert terrain, and then hours of nothing, and either way, at the end of the day, a few more bunny runs. Would you care to explain that gap?"

"It takes a long time to get down the mountain from the

top of the West Peak when you ski the way I do." Melanie crossed her arms before her, which didn't look particularly intimidating with her breasts sticking out over. He'd enjoyed her breasts greatly once, and so, he supposed, had Ulf.

"There's only one run you could have possibly survived coming down from the top of the West Peak, and there's no real reason to be teaching on Killy's Knees when there are similar slopes with less danger, all accessible from the lower lift. However—" He paused for effect. "—there is no small cabin, suitable for a love nest, halfway down the mountain, though there is a very pretty one at the top. And what about the days where you didn't take the Scott lifts? Where were you two then, dear? Upstairs?"

"Certainly not!" she flared.

"You certainly were, Melanie. You see"—James Underwood spoke even more softly—"I've already talked to Lupe. That's the downside of having a housekeeper." He let her think about that for a moment and hoped she would figure out that what she paid the woman for silence, he'd doubled for the truth. "I suppose I could have had a friend in the State Department get Ulf's visa revoked if he were still alive, but that wouldn't solve the basic problem between you and me, would it?"

"There is no problem, and I can't believe you think there is!" Tears started to drip down her face, tears he didn't believe for a moment, because he'd taken her away from Hollywood when he married her. "Lupe would say anything at all to keep her job!"

"All she had to say was the truth. Whatever it was. And since Rudi Gernsbach had something similar to say when I confronted him, I'd say there is a problem."

He waited for her protestation of "Who's Rudi Gernsbach?" but that question never came.

"He was rather anxious to tell me everything I wished to

know, in exchange for keeping Alpenschlössl running. Which he may, for now." Underwood figured he'd do something about Rudi and his little school of skiing sex partners once he'd sorted out his personal problems, since it was clear that the only instructor who wasn't happy about the arrangement no longer worked there—Kurt. His Alpenschlössl season pass did a normal instructor pattern up and down the mountain, because he hadn't given it back when he fled Rudi for the Wapiti Creek Ski School.

"So, Melanie, why don't you tell me the truth about the two of you?" Underwood looked sadly at the woman for whom he'd turned his life upside down eight years ago.

"He loved me." She sat up straighter, tears forgotten, back to defiance.

"I suppose that's why he was at the cabin with a man the day he died." Underwood smiled sadly at the start that revelation gave her. "I loved you too, Melanie. Enough to leave Claire and my children for you. I hurt people I cared about to be with you, so I might even deserve this. But I'm not going to pretend we can put things back together."

"People do. People fix their marriages all the time." Now her huge brown eyes fixed limpidly on him. He thought of her one speaking part in the movies that never led to more.

"If I thought this was a real marriage, we might. Now I think it was more of a business association, where you got to be Mrs. Underwood and live a wealthy life, and I got to have the most beautiful lady on my arm and in my bed. But you made a side deal." Underwood reached into his hip pocket and produced a set of keys and some credit cards.

"I reviewed the prenuptial agreement. I also emailed you a scanned copy, if you don't recall what you did with your original. So, here's your new house keys; the address is on the tag. It's a two-bedroom condo in the new development on Elk Road. This one was already furnished and decorated. You can live in it or sell it, your choice. You keep the Mercedes SUV. It's less than a year old and has less than seven thousand miles. Your new credit cards." He handed her the plastic. "The credit limit isn't what you're used to, but I'm not paying the tab anymore. The bank account in your name has your yearly stipend there and ready. Use it wisely, because you can't come back to the well. We'll move your clothes and things in the morning."

Melanie half stood and growled, "You think you can just throw me out like that?"

"Yes, Melanie, I do. I am. It's what we agreed to before we got married. You thought it was generous enough then, though I guess you've gotten a taste of the lush life since." Underwood rubbed his temples a moment, blessing a truly talented lawyer for assembling the prenup. "Try and fight it—you'll end up with less."

She didn't sit down. "What about child support?"

"You plan to pay me?" He looked into her eyes with the determination that had built a ski resort empire, and let her see he meant it. She gasped and sat back with a thump. "Todd and Gracie stay with me, Mel. You'd just ignore them for the next pair of broad shoulders attached to an intriguing accent." He wasn't going to mention that the odds of her finding a new gig as trophy wife were markedly lower this time around, and would be lower yet with the children in tow. "You can see them as often as you want."

He rose to his full six feet and looked down on his stunned, soon-to-be ex-wife. "The season lift ticket you keep, and you can have another every year 'til you drop dead, if you like, but you don't have to take any more lessons unless you want to." He let her savor a moment of reprieve before he let the last brick

drop. "I have no interest in how well the former Mrs. Underwood skis."

Melanie sat at the table seething, long after Underwood left the
room. It was going to be a long, hard descent from being the
wife of the man who controlled four of the ritziest resorts in
North America to being his ex, because she had few illusions
about what was going to happen to her social circles. No more
head tables at charity events, no more giggly afternoons with
visiting celebrities who'd come to enjoy Wapiti Creek's fabulous
slopes and elegant shops. No more dinners with Olympic-level
athletes. Trying to pick up the shreds of what had been a not-
very-successful acting career eight years ago was out of the question. She'd been one of hundreds of beautiful, hopeful actresses
whose credits read "Woman in crowd" or "Receptionist" for
screen times that had lasted a few seconds.

Why wouldn't he even consider trying to patch things up?
Why did he have to go straight to a divorce? She was beautiful,
desirable—he shouldn't be angry that someone else had agreed
with him! He had his damned mountains—why shouldn't she
have Ulf? Oh, this was all his fault! Her life was totally in shambles, and there was no need for it!

When the housekeeper stepped in to clear the table,
Melanie turned to her with a snarl and hurled a plate. Screaming, "Lying bitch!" and fleeing before the china even shattered
against the fieldstone fireplace, Melanie ran upstairs, not sure if
she wanted to beg James to reconsider or to fling something at
his head. The door to the master suite was blocked with a large
moving box. She stopped short as he came to place an armload
of cashmere into it. Behind him she could see empty drawers

hanging open and a blank space on the dresser where pictures and perfume bottles had been.

"I'm sleeping in the blue room tonight, Mel." He turned back to the dresser and opened a drawer that contained a lot of expensive size-four jeans.

"This is our room, James." She brought the tears back for him. "I want to sleep here. With you."

He peered into the drawer, inspecting the contents and missing the show completely. "I'm not sleeping on that bed again." He placed the jeans on top of the sweaters in the big packing box, filling it. He wove the top flaps together and pushed the box to one side. There were several other big boxes leaning flat against the bed, waiting to be opened and loaded. Melanie watched him pack away her old life.

"James, please, can't we try again?" She let her bottom lip quiver. "I'm sorry, I truly am sorry. Please let's don't throw our life together away."

"It's already gone, Melanie." James turned to her, his voice low and tired. He gestured jerkily around the room, his motion amplified by the large mirrors on the wall and over the dresser. "How can I be in this room with you and not wonder if you're looking over my shoulder to see his reflection?" Abruptly he stood taller, again becoming the corporate cutthroat she latched onto those years ago, though it was her throat at risk this time. "Don't just stand there, pack something."

Silently, she went to the closet for an armload of shoeboxes. So he was determined to shed her like an unwanted asset? Treat her like a piece of property that didn't fit into his portfolio anymore? Screw her life up beyond recognition?

She'd go. But she'd make him regret it.

FOUR

I watched a skier in a burgundy patrol jacket, twin to my own, swing expertly around the chain barrier to the lift line. I'd been about to yell "Single!" to collect a partner for the chairlift, but Kim would ride with me and we could talk patrol business on the way to the top of the West Peak. She waved at me and skied up to the front of the line. The patrols didn't wait turns; we were needed on the slopes.

"I just came off Sundance." Kim named an intermediate run once we were seated in the chairlift. "A couple of snowboarders are riding kind of wild—cutting back and forth in front of each other. Possibly they've been drinking. I think one of them is that guy from the robot action flick that opened right before Christmas, Cal Somebody-or-other. Black and silver jacket; his buddy's in some loud blue Hawaiian-print pants." Great. We patrols loved inebriated celebrities. I had liked this particular celebrity a great deal, one vodka-fueled evening last season. So he'd brought a companion this time. Cal probably didn't remember my name.

"So, how did Cereal Bowl look?" Kim pulled her fleece

headband off and tried to bring some order to her curly brown mop. I held her poles as she waged the losing battle.

"Not bad. I only had to rescue one loose ski for some guy who'd done an eggbeater." I shook my head. He'd gone down in a whirl of arms, legs, skis, and poles about a third of the way down the easy slope. "He said he wasn't hurt, though he managed to get the inside of his goggles full of snow."

"How far did you have to climb to get back to him?" Every patrol chased equipment down the mountain now and then. Kim got the headband back on and retrieved her poles. She didn't look much different than when she started.

"About twenty yards. He was grateful." I'd gotten a blinding smile and a genuine thank you when I pulled him up off the snow to put the errant ski back on, not the muttered politeness of wounded machismo.

"He should have been. You could have made him come down to you." Going down a mountain on one ski was beyond a lot of people's skills, though I'd seen Jorey Taylor do it in a race. Kim grinned slyly. "So, was he cute?"

"Kim!" I did not want another assault on my social life, or lack thereof, from her, and I was stuck on this lift for a while yet. "I don't flirt with the skiers." I used to, but I got cured of that when Rudi Gernsbach tried to hire me for Alpenschlössl. What a wake-up call that had been. I didn't need any more one-night stands or fly-by-night relationships, and I was sick of being used like a ski lift or hot tub, just another resort amenity. That was all gone with last season's snows—I was ready for something, someone real.

"More fool you then," she shot back, as if she understood. "Was he cute or not?"

"Well…not cute, really." The smile was wide, the cleft chin strong, and the brown eyes under straight dark brows were warm, if a bit shy, as he cleaned the snow out of his goggles. Good-looking, more like, but I wasn't going to tell her that. Also probably someone I wouldn't see again, a stranger met once. "And leave the social life alone."

"Nuh uh, not anymore." She made a face at me. "Mark McAvoy, you are officially being tossed back into the dating pool. Julie, Chelsea, and I are sick and tired of you mooning around. Your social life has been nonexistent except for us. You've been alone and unhappy, and even if Jake perked you back up for about a day and a half...." She paused, maybe considering the effect of me continuing to pursue Jake on our group's dynamic. "Anyway, he's not an option, so we're going to find you someone who is."

I began to silently curse having a circle of concerned friends. This could get ugly. "Kim, no. Stop. No."

She waved to someone coming down the run next to the lift. "You don't have to fall in love or anything; you just need someone who makes you smile when he walks into the room. And since you just hang around with the bunch of us, we're going to get more people into the bunch." She grinned at me as if she'd just had the best idea ever. "So we're having a potluck at your place Thursday."

Oh, hell no. "We can't, Kim! I own one chair and about two plates!" She was wrong about the not needing to fall in love part too; I just didn't want her directing how it happened.

"Doesn't matter. We have paper plates, and we'll sit on the floor. There's lots of room—we can play Twister." She giggled. "Tidy up and expect everyone around seven."

Tidy.... I groaned. "No, Kim, how about your place? I'll come, I promise."

"Heard that before, Mark, and you never showed. This time

we're dragging the party to you. Thursday, seven." She sat back after delivering this crushing pronouncement.

"You can't...."

"Can and will. Did. Already invited people. Scrub the bathroom. Guys always forget the bathroom." Her eyes got really big behind her goggles. "Oh no. Mark, when was the last time you cleaned the bathroom?"

I shrugged. "I don't remember."

She looked sick. "You don't remember. How about the kitchen?"

"I don't cook much."

Green didn't look good on her. "Does the carpet crunch?"

"I don't eat potato chips in the living room." I sounded defensive, I knew, but I really didn't spend a lot of time being domestic. There was no one but me to make a mess, and I was hardly ever there, but....

"Do you even remember the last time you vacuumed?"

"I don't have a vacuum."

"You are an idiot slob, and no wonder you live alone. Mark, there's a vacuum on each floor that belongs to the building. No excuses, buddy. You are going to get that place clean, because otherwise no one is going to be willing to walk through your front door, let alone the bedroom door." She whacked my thigh with the side of her fist.

"You are a busybody, woman. Did anybody ever mention that?" The top of the hill couldn't come soon enough for me.

"Yes. It's one of my better qualities." She lifted the safety bar on the chairlift. "See you tonight," she said, sailing off the unloading platform.

I swung toward Prospector, a narrow intermediate run, and radioed in my intention to patrol. Wait, tonight? It was Tuesday, not Thursday, and it wasn't our usual night to go to

McTavish's. I scanned the terrain ahead, going slowly through the slender passage in the trees, alert to trouble. She had to have been distracted, and I had time to convince someone else to act as host. In the meantime, I'd enjoy my work on the barely groomed slope that had surely tripped up someone.

Dinner was something in a takeout carton that had tasted a lot better the first time around. I threw the white cardboard into the trash, which didn't quite overflow, and thought gloomily about Kim's questions earlier. When had I cleaned the bathroom last? Where was the cleaning stuff? Probably in some logical place like under the sink, but I didn't bother looking for it. I wasn't hosting this potluck. Maybe Devon or Gabe wanted the crowd. Or Jake and Kurt. Their battered green couch could seat four, and they had a table. I'd knock on a couple doors and pawn this project off.

I opened the door—but I shut it a lot faster. Was there another way out of this apartment? The sliding glass door to the tiny balcony, maybe, but I was three floors up and didn't think I could get down the icy building without some equipment. I could do a Spider-Man to the next balcony, but that neighbor would leave me in the cold as payback for waking him with my nightmares. Maybe I could hide? Pretend I wasn't here?

"Mark! Hey, Mark!" Rapping knuckles on the wood announced I was trapped. "We're here!" Kim's voice floated through the door.

She *had* meant "tonight." And "we" meant she brought help; I'd seen the terrible trio marching down the hall before I shut the door, and got a glimpse of the weaponry they were carrying.

"We know you're in there, Mark!" Chelsea called. "Come on!" My partner on the snow conditions team, Marty, swore she was the sweetest thing and was planning to marry her, but she sounded more bossy than sweet just now. It sounded like she was thumping on the door with the handle of her broom. If I didn't answer, would she get on and fly away?

"We're here to help, Mark," Julie coaxed. She and Chelsea both taught skiing, but Julie got the littles, and probably used that particular voice on them all day long.

Kim would make a bigger scene if I left them standing, so I gathered my courage and opened the door. Finding these three lovely ladies on the doorstep was probably the fantasy of half the guys living in our building, but I didn't expect to enjoy their company tonight. "Hi there." I tried to keep the deer-in-the-headlights look off my face. "What brings you here?"

"Present for you." Kim marched through the door first, shoving a toilet brush into my hand. "Did you get started without us?" She stood in the middle of my nearly empty living room and surveyed with hands on her hips. "If you did, I can't tell where. Bathroom?"

"Uh, no." I stared stupidly at the brush in my hand. "Not yet." Maybe I could stave off the invasion. No such luck. Chelsea stuck her head in the kitchen as Julie started picking up magazines off the living room floor. Oh, no. *Those* magazines.

"Geez, Mark, these belong in the bedroom." She brandished one of my favorites, giggling. I grabbed it away from her, hugging it to my chest protectively, hoping my face wasn't as red as it felt.

"We had an election and you won," Kim informed me. "You are now president of the bathroom cleaning association. Go visit your constituency. We'll get busy out here."

"What? Why?" That sounded whiny even to me.

"Because this place needs some love. Take this." Kim handed me a bottle of cleanser and a rag from her bucket of supplies. "*We* aren't going to scrub whiskers and crap out of the bathroom." She squirted into the bucket. "You'll want these, too." Rubber gloves sailed toward me.

"*Ew!*" floated out of the kitchen. "What have you been doing in here?" Instead of answering that, I bolted into the bathroom with my new cleaning things.

One good look around convinced me that the girls had a point. If I hid in here and worked diligently, they wouldn't come in and criticize what a single guy could do to an innocent bathroom. The crud hadn't registered twenty minutes ago, but now I questioned if the sink really was white underneath the layers. I brushed my teeth in here this morning, but the rubber gloves seemed like a good idea. I scrubbed while trying to both hear and ignore what they were saying.

"Oh, gross!" and "Blech!" figured prominently, with "I need the broom in here," and once a shriek of "Is it dead?"

That brought my head straight up out of the bathtub, where white was beginning to be the dominant color again.

"That's a hairbrush." Chelsea had run to diagnose the corpse. She should talk—her long, strawberry blond waves probably shed every bit as bad as my hair. "Take care of this, please." She brought it into the bathroom, holding it like a dead mouse between two fingers, and placed it on the freshly cleaned counter, where it did look rather shaggy and decrepit. I dropped it in the wastebasket, slightly grossed out myself. "Looking better in here by the minute." She smiled at me with encouragement and headed back to the kitchen.

"Hey, did anyone ask Jim?" Chelsea called out. I wondered who Jim was.

"He asked if he could bring his new boyfriend." Kim's answer cut off the wondering.

"Oh. How about Carl?"

"Had plans." Great. Two possibles down the tubes. I flushed the can and sprinkled more cleanser around.

"Do we need to clean the refrigerator?"

The obscene *pop* of the gasket unsticking from the frame answered the question for her. When exactly had I spilled that Coke?

"There's not much in here. The milk hasn't expired." Would serve Kim right if it had, and I imagined her getting a rancid whiff as payback for interfering. "What the heck do you live on, Mark?" she shouted from the kitchen.

"Takeout, baloney sandwiches, and cornflakes!" I bellowed back. Flushing the can again drowned out whatever criticism she might have of my diet. At least things were looking better in here.

"Oh, Mark." Julie came to the door and propped the broom against the wall. "You really are a case in point for why guys shouldn't be alone." I looked up at her and away, not wanting to see the pity in her brown eyes. She rested her hand gently on my shoulder. "You've gotten so thin. We've neglected you."

"No, not really." Restaurant meals paid for by others weren't a steady part of my diet anymore, that was all. I shut the lid on the can and got off my knees to sit on it; it should pass Kim the sanitation cop's inspection by now. She came close enough that I could rest my head against her waist and put my arms around her hips. "I just wish…. Julie, I'm just tired of being alone. The guys I used to date—being alone is better, but still…." She stroked my hair and then threw the end of one dark brown braid over her shoulder because it was batting the top of my head. "I miss little things like hugs. Good mornings." Sex, but she could figure that out for herself.

"Your girlfriend squad can only make up for so much of that, I suppose." Julie wasn't the only one of the three I hugged on a regular basis, just to be touched. Marty didn't mind. He knew I wasn't going to poach Chelsea, and the two of them were probably the best friends I had next to Julie and Kim. For all their bossiness, the girls were a damned important part of my life. Julie massaged my shoulders. "You do know that we're going to have to approve of whoever you date, Mark."

"I want my friends to like him, but 'approve'?" I stood up so I could look down into her eyes, but she hugged me close and wouldn't let me admonish her with a stern look.

"Yup," she mumbled into my chest, "because he should be someone who can be our friend, too. You don't exist in a vacuum—you have friends." I'd kept my previous social activities as far away from my friends as I could, and that had gotten old even before Ruci made his offer.

She suddenly stiffened and drew away from me, exclaiming in laughing horror, "Ick! You still have those rubber gloves on!"

"They're a fetish for some people." I flexed my fingers at her and leered. She took two steps back.

"Not for you, or you'd clean the bathroom more often!" She wrinkled up her nose. "You can have the mop when Kim's done with it. I'm going to go find the vacuum." She handed me the broom and dustpan before disappearing.

"I already tried, Julie." Chelsea interrupted her errand. "Allan has it. He said he'd bring it over when he's done."

Whoever Allan was, he was clearly more domestic than me.

"Okay, what's left to do?"

"The mirrors are all that's left, I think," Kim said over her shoulder. She came to the bathroom door to assess my progress. "Hey, this is looking like a real bathroom again."

I dipped the mop into the bucket she'd just set down and looked smug. "Of course. I do good work."

"When you do it." She did that sideways head tilt that made her look like a poodle. "Which had better be often, because next time we're going to sit around and supervise."

"Yeah, *this* time we're helping," Chelsea agreed, and a deep voice answered her.

"How does Mark rate the help?"

His question made me step out to see who went with that almost-familiar sound. The speaker hadn't let go of the vacuum he'd wheeled down the hall, I saw, and then I looked at his face. I'd seen him somewhere, though I didn't recognize him as a neighbor. He had to live in the building, though, or he wouldn't be here bearing appliances.

"We're making him clean up his act," Kim announced.

That stung. "Actually, they're my harem, and I've put them to work," I suggested loftily, sending them into gales of laughter and snorting, which I tried to ignore. "Hi. Thanks for bringing that over." Where had I seen him? "Here, girls, get busy!" I pretended to crack a whip, forgetting I was still wearing yellow rubber gloves, which spoiled the effect. He grinned, and I suddenly remembered where I'd seen him. "You must be Allan?"

"Yeah, Allan Tengerdie. Down the hall in 345. You must be the fortunate Mark?" He stuck his hand out. I put mine out but didn't take his, not with my foul rubber glove still on.

"Mark McAvoy." I pulled the glove off and completed the introduction. "Don't know about fortunate—I have this set of slave drivers directing my evening." He laughed at the slit-eyed glare I cast over my shoulder. "They've decided that nothing will do but that we have a party in here."

"Sounds like fun." The grin I'd seen last on the Cereal Bowl faded. Allan was the guy whose ski I'd retrieved earlier today. The cleft chin and the squarish face were the same beyond a doubt. His slightly stocky body hadn't been apparent under his parka and bibs, though I'd noticed then he was about four inches shorter than my six foot one.

"What are you doing Thursday?" Kim wanted to know.

"Once I get the orders out and the paperwork sorted, nothing, really." His grin was back; it lit up his eyes.

"Good. Potluck here at seven." Kim stole the vacuum cleaner from between me and Allan and headed to the bedroom with it. Good thinking—if she was being domestic, I was less likely to yell at her, and certainly not over the roar of the machine.

"Sounds like a plan. I'll be here. If that's okay with you." He checked with me, correctly deducing that Kim was working my nerves.

"Yeah. Come." I liked the smile.

"Potluck, huh." He looked thoughtful. "See you then." He left with a little wave and shut the door behind him.

"Well, he didn't ask to bring anyone with him," Chelsea commented.

"Yeah, but he's a guy. How much do you want to bet we're going to have twenty bags of chips and a ton of beer, and no real food unless we cook it?" Julie quirked her mouth. "Like last time?"

"I will make something real, okay?" Two of the bags of chips and some of the beer had come with me to the last potluck. I had no idea what qualified as real that I could make, but I'd figure something out. "Do any of you know him?"

"He lives down the hall with Randi Hooper." Chelsea bundled up the trash.

"Well, maybe he makes good conversation." If he lived with a Randy, that took him right out of consideration.

"I don't know him, but I do know Randi, and trust me, Mark," Chelsea said with a wink, "she isn't interested in him. Hey! Maybe he can talk her into cooking something for the potluck. She's a chef down at the Antlers Hotel."

"Should we invite her, too?" Kim wondered. She'd stuck her head back in after Allan left, curiosity getting the better of her self-preservation.

"Not this time. She's working. She can't come to much that isn't on a Monday. I'll try to catch her and find out more about Mystery Boy." Chelsea took the trash bag toward the door. "I'll dump this on my way out. Looking good in here, Mark."

I thanked her and watched her leave, wondering what she'd learn about Allan. The one thing I did know was that he was an inept skier. That was too bad, because I really liked the smile.

FIVE

The sound of doors opening and shutting again made me think of the rush before classes in a college dorm as people up and down the hall headed out to work. I'd be one of them in a moment after I dumped the contents of the bowl, currently riding around in the microwave, into my Thermos. The red-and-white can flew into the trash. The kitchen looked really good after the girls, bless them, scrubbed it down last night. It looked good enough to cook in. Too bad I didn't cook.

The bathroom no longer looked like it would try to slay me with typhoid every time I showered, and the carpet had revealed itself to be half-dead beige plush instead of brown crumbs. Instead of resenting Kim and the crew for meddling, as I had last night, I could be grateful to them this morning. My life didn't have to be a sorry shambles in all directions. I was even sleeping better. I hadn't dreamed in several days, since Kurt and Jake had taken me in.

Professionally, my life was just fine. This was my fifth season of patrolling, and even if it wasn't something to be doing for the next forty years, I enjoyed it. Aside from the occasional need to pull bodies out of the snow—okay, just once—it was a great way to make a living. Ski all day, be alert, help those who needed it, and trigger the occasional avalanche. Marty and I were the snow conditions experts, which meant we got to shoot the big guns from time to time. Gotta love a job that lets a guy play with a howitzer.

We'd head up to the West Peak today, because a fresh snowfall and a lot of wind made a few of the slopes up there risky. Snowboarders loved the cornices, but a fallen cornice could bring the whole slope down if weak layers caused the snow pack to separate. Marty and I would take some core samples and decide if we needed to close a couple of runs. That all had to be done in the two hours before the lifts opened to the public.

I threw the soup into the bag and grabbed my burgundy patrol parka, which I'd put on once I reached the patrol hut, and headed out. Marching down the hall, I realized how few of my neighbors I really knew. I had names to go with only one or two doors in this long hallway. Allan could have been living under my nose for a long time, and I wouldn't have known it, though if I'd lined up for the vacuum more often, I might have met him a year ago. He was on this floor was all I knew. Time to make more of an effort to meet the neighbors. As much as I hated to admit it, Kim had a point about my limited social circle.

Just before I reached the central stairs, my attention was arrested by a figure emerging from a door on the other wing. Laden with beige blobs in bags, the man staggered out and tried to pull the door shut behind him without losing any of his burden, but the blobs would swing out and knock the door away. It was kind of comical but probably frustrating. In my new spirit of sociability, I kept going past the stairs to give him a hand. I wouldn't have been so social if I hadn't recognized him; it was Allan.

"Need a hand?" I reached out to the door at the same time he did, the blobs swinging like pendulums against the door again.

"No, oh—" He turned with an irritated snort. Though once he saw me, the corners of his mouth turned up. "Yeah. Guess I do. Thanks."

"What are these things you're fighting with?" I had to ask about the blobs, which hung in plastic bags.

"Dough for cinnamon rolls. I brought it home because my kitchen gets too chilly at night for it to rise properly." He took a firmer grip on the tops of the plastic bags.

"That's a lot of cinnamon rolls." My mouth started watering. It had been a long time since I had a cinnamon roll, and even in their unfinished state, the rolls whispered to me. I didn't reach for the door.

"They're on the menu today. What are you swinging around?" He gestured with his chin toward my bag, making his blobs sway.

"Baloney sandwich and some soup."

"Did it come out of a can?" he asked suspiciously.

"Yeah. Isn't that the usual source for soup?"

"Not for good soup. Come on." He pushed the still open door with his foot and went back in and dropped the dough on the kitchen table. I followed him into the apartment, wondering what he was planning. "Give me that." I handed over my lunch bag.

A glass bowl from the fridge landed in the microwave to heat while Allan pulled my Thermos out and dumped the contents down the drain. "Yuck. You'll like homemade corn chowder much better."

"The kitchen seems warm enough for cinnamon rolls." I sniffed the luscious aroma that wafted from the microwave. Why was he dragging the dough out of the kitchen here? My craving for a roll increased.

"Not this one. I lease space in a restaurant kitchen, since I need the commercial setup. The building is between restaurants, you could say; the last guy failed, and they don't have anyone new in, so I have it for now. Since I only need it in the daytime, I can turn the heat down at night." He leaned against the counter to talk while the chowder heated.

"Places in this town don't stay empty long," I observed, eyeing the dough as if it might grow spirals with brown sugar and cinnamon inside from the strength of my longing. I couldn't resist giving one bag of dough a poke. It sprang back when my finger withdrew.

"The location is bad for the tourist trade, and the guy didn't want to try for the staff. Someone with more sense will come along presently, and I'll lose the facilities. I'm saving for a place of my own with the right setup, probably down valley, and I need to do it before someone else takes over, because I sure can't work from here." Allan looked around the little kitchen dismissively.

"Why not?" Aside from the fact that the whole apartment reeked of cigarette smoke. There wasn't enough cinnamon in the world to cover up that scent. I didn't think he'd generated it; I hadn't gotten more than a hint of the smoke last night.

"I make meals for seventy to eighty people a day, so I need the commercial kitchen, or the health department will shut me down, quite aside from not enough counter space." The pride in his voice was evident. "Almost Home Catering, that's me." The microwave beeped, signaling Allan to pour the yellow chunky soup into my thermos.

"I've seen your fliers around." And wished that I could afford the service, too. Someone to make dinner and bring it by, so no one had to cook or go out to eat, sounded heavenly.

"Good. The tourists keep me busy in the winter. Summer, well, we'll see." He returned my lunch bag and gathered up his blobs. "Gotta go turn this into rolls." I followed him out and shut the door for him.

"Hey, you cook, I need some advice." The opportunity wasn't going to get any better. "I have been told in no uncertain terms that I have to do 'real food' for tomorrow, and I have no idea what to make. It has to be easy."

Allan laughed. "Easy, right. Get a bag of potatoes, scrub them, and shove them in the oven for an hour at three hundred fifty degrees. A tub of butter, a tub of sour cream, you have real food."

I laughed, thinking of Kim's face when she saw what I would put on the table. "It doesn't get any easier than that. Thanks."

Once outside, he headed for the eastbound shuttle, but I had to get on the westbound. I watched him get on, with one last smile for me. I waved before crossing the street to the other shuttle, thinking that Kim's little plan had borne fruit already.

Homemade soup and cinnamon rolls—why had I not tracked this man down a year ago?

SIX

Marty helped me examine the cores of snow we'd cut out of the slope. "I think it's going to hold."

"You sure? I'd rather not have to trigger," I admitted once we finished. "But we could have the snow cats out here and have this run open again by ten."

"This slope would have been groomed again by opening if you hadn't been so late getting here," Marty groused. "But I don't think we need to do it."

"Let's take one more set," I suggested. The events of the previous November made me jumpy, but the last set of cores suggested that the snow wasn't in danger of shearing off a slab. It would be much better to do it before the slopes opened if we had to start an avalanche, after all.

"One more. I don't want another chewing-out like last time if we have a slide during lift hours again." Marty skied down another ten yards and drove the corer between his skis. He said "chewing-out," but we both knew he meant "another death."

His avalanche vest bulked him up and made it awkward to slice down to the base. I joined him and leaned my weight into the handles, making the corer bite into the snow. In the back country we'd have dug a pit, but we couldn't disrupt the ski trail like that. Together we examined the crystals at the different depths, and agreed that today there was no need to close the run.

"So what kept you?" Marty asked on the way down the hill. We were on Helium Heights, a black diamond expert slope, so conversation went in fits and starts in our turns to and away from each other.

"Stopped to talk to someone," I got out on a near pass, and then pulled up at the left side of the slope. A tree had fallen and would need to be removed by a snowcat, but we'd mark the hazard. Marty pulled up with me, and we strung some red plastic tape around the branches. He radioed the news into the patrol hut, where Ben agreed to send a cat out.

"Someone important enough to make you late?" Marty asked pointedly.

"Not sure yet." Food was nice, and Allan seemed interested, but the big question was, did he lean my way? There was nothing that pinged the gaydar hard enough for certainty, no mannerism or tone of voice that said I'd have to succeed with him, or fail, on my own merits instead of having lost just for being male. For all I knew, he fed everyone who looked hungry.

"Anyone I know?" Marty tied off the red tape, and I cut it with my jackknife. The wind nipped my fingers because I couldn't open the knife with gloves on. It would take a while for my hand to warm again, even in the glove. Seemed like I was cold all the time now, something that hadn't been a problem before. I used to be better insulated.

"Probably not. You'll meet him tomorrow." If Chelsea didn't know him, it seemed unlikely that Marty would.

"Right. You have the matchmakers on your case." He

should know; Kim and Julie introduced him to Chelsea a couple of years ago, and they'd been inseparable ever since. He pushed his prescription sunglasses farther up his nose and swung down the slope again.

"Yeah." I was talking to empty air, so I followed him. At least I was following a guy who'd gotten good results from Kim and Julie's meddling.

I didn't have to drag anyone down the mountain in a stretcher that morning, so it was a glorious blue-sky day of skiing, marred only by an ugly incident with a drunken skier who came away from our encounter without his lift ticket. I hated doing that, but if it's a matter of one person being angry or a lot of people being endangered, it's an easy call.

Our usual table in the staff hut was filling up when I got there at lunch: Jake, Kurt, Julie, and Gabe were already sitting and eating, and Chelsea was getting napkins. Several noses began to sniff appreciatively when I got my thermos open.

"What's that?" Gabe asked, staring pointedly at the container.

"Corn chowder. Homemade." I spooned in a mouthful, thick with potato and corn, rich with smoky bacon. Oh, wonderful stuff.

"Whose home?" Julie knew quite well it wasn't mine.

"Allan's. I ran into him again this morning." If I shoveled it in as fast as I wanted to, the chowder would be gone too soon, so I forced myself to eat slowly. The canned stuff that went down the drain this morning did not deserve the title of soup.

"Taste?" Julie waved her spoon suggestively, then dipped it into the reluctantly offered container. Her face turned blissful. The gang looked at her and turned to me, suddenly predatory.

"Guys! This is my lunch!" Cuddling the thermos into my

chest defensively, I fended off the instant forest of waving spoons. "If everyone gets tastes, there won't be anything left."

"We don't have to worry about real food for tomorrow if this is what he makes," Julie said, before dreamily licking her lips.

"Does that mean you'll let me bring chips?" Gabe asked over his sandwich.

"Maybe." Her arch look suggested she'd let him do a few other things too.

"I can always bring cookies instead," he concluded, looking satisfied that he wouldn't have to stretch himself in the kitchen. Julie shook a playful finger at him, which he grabbed.

I finished the chowder, savoring every mouthful, wondering why Allan had taken the time to change out my lunch this morning. Did he believe in getting to a man's heart through his stomach? Or did he just loathe canned soup?

My day ended when the lifts closed and I'd done a final sweep for stray skiers. My slopes were clear, so I headed home, wanting a hot shower and a warm meal. Nothing I'd eat tonight would begin to match lunch—the options were a frozen cardboard pizza or going out again, which was getting a little hard on the budget. Cardboard won, but once out of the shower, I had a better thought. Maybe Allan had more chowder? Maybe I shouldn't be such a mooch. Definitely I should thank him. That virtuous thought, coupled with hope that if properly thanked, he'd offer more, propelled me down the hall.

No one answered my knock, leaving my virtue unrewarded.

The pizza had all the charm of this morning's discarded soup. Days on the mountain required fuel of some sort, but there really had to be a better source than the freezer case at the market. I'd have to break down and learn to cook, because I sure couldn't depend on random handouts, and there was no way I was going back to dining out on other people's titanium credit cards.

It was early yet, I thought, too early to turn in but too late to show up on someone's doorstep, even if I felt like getting up out of the easy chair. Julie had stacked the magazines neatly in the rack, but I didn't want *Velo News* or *Wired* tonight, and she'd moved the good stuff out of the living room. Or had she? I shuffled through the rack and found one she missed.

I'd had a couple of glorious evenings thinking about Jake, which I put aside reluctantly once it was clear how bonded he was with Kurt, and a few more thinking about what had happened when I'd taken refuge with him and Kurt. That, too, I'd put aside, a memory to be enjoyed at rare intervals, because thinking about that would send me downstairs again, and I'd promised not to do that. The impersonal arousal I'd get from the pictures was the best I had.

The perfectly airbrushed muscles and penises in various stages of erection were usually enough to keep me happy, but tonight they were only enough to get me started. The untouchable beauty and manufactured sultry glances had a lot in common with the canned soup and frozen pizza: good enough if nothing else was available. I wouldn't have pulled Allan out of a lineup for his good looks, but he'd cared enough to do me a kindness.

More than enough men had chosen me for being good-looking and willing; I'd let them be my ticket into the clubs and restaurants. Most of them had whined when I'd gone to work in the early morning. All of them were gone like smoke, back to their real lives, after a vacation in the mountains.

Allan, though—he'd talked to me. He'd fed me. He'd treated me pleasantly and asked nothing in return. He hadn't taken it directly to sex. He lived here; he had ties, friends, a business to keep him from disappearing. He—well, he was real.

The magazine fell to the floor, and I didn't reach after it, thinking instead of Allan's smile and wondering how he'd fit into my arms. I could tease him with my tongue in the cleft of his chin before trailing it down his neck. He'd be a generous lover, too, he had to be. He'd fill my mouth and my senses, he'd.... I'd pulled my cock out of my pants and stroked it, my hand moving with every new thought. The orgasm soon rolled through me, pulling groans from deep in my throat.

It was wonderful, but I'd really based an awful lot on one bowl of soup.

SEVEN

Next morning, I was halfway out the door when a soft thud arrested my attention. Something in a grocery bag hung from the knob, thumping gently on the door. The cinnamon roll could have come from only one source, and Marty was just going to have to wait for me while I finished it.

That roll was every bit as good as I'd imagined yesterday, when it was a doughy shadow of the cinnamon bliss I now licked from my fingertips. Moaning through my mouthful reminded me that I'd made these same noises last night while thinking of Allan. That man was just dominating my thoughts, and I'd barely had a proper conversation with him. He'd be here tonight—I'd have to really get to know him.

A few more bags hung from doorknobs up and down the hall, marking those who stood high enough in Allan's affections to rate an early morning treat. I considered stealing them all.

Melanie sat down hard on the queen-size bed that she'd sleep in alone for the foreseeable future. The elegance of the new condo left her unmoved: what others would have paid hundreds of thousands of dollars for was a place of banishment for her. Strewn around the bedroom were the boxes that James had filled with designer clothes and boutique accessories, still not put away. She hadn't packed much that night. She'd fled to the bathroom but had cried instead of collecting her makeup and toiletries, and now would have to sort out what James had swept into boxes. He'd handled the glass bottles and compacts carefully, but he'd been determined to remove all traces of her presence, not retiring to the blue bedroom until long after midnight. She'd tried to join him, but he'd locked the door.

It had been a long, cold night, alone in the king-size bed where she'd spent most of her marriage, warmed either by her husband or by her lover. Ulf had heated her enough to spend the hours on the slopes, and she'd hoped that one day she could lie down next to him without wondering how long before she'd put the silky long johns back on and get her cheeks pinked up by the temperatures. Passion didn't flush her in quite the same way.

No lush life now, with or without Ulf, she moped; she'd done the math and realized that her yearly stipend was about what she'd spent on her own clothing last year. James had relieved her of the necessity of working, but her standard of living had just taken a nosedive. She'd planned to outlive him and enjoy all the fruits of his real estate empire, but he'd proven annoyingly resilient, which she should have expected. How could she have realistically screwed him into the grave when he could ski as well as any of his patrollers?

The mountain hadn't obliged her by slaying her husband, taking her lover instead. She'd read the reports and grieved, which had made James's unkind remark about black underwear sting. Why couldn't he have gone to investigate what his snow conditions team was doing, setting off a slide so late in the day? Just because she couldn't ski well didn't mean she ignored the rhythms of the resort, and such things should have been done before the lifts ever opened.

Why? she wondered the morning she'd moved in here. Had James somehow planned that, as ruthlessly as he had planned her removal from his house and his life? And if he had, he should pay for that as well. That thought hadn't left her, and now she had plans of her own in motion.

News of her fall from grace hadn't spread widely yet, something that worked to her advantage, she'd decided as she looked through her address book. One lawyer she had discarded as a possibility at once: he did far too much work for James. Yet another had been welcome in their home as a friend, though she knew precisely whose friend, and it wasn't hers. In fact, there were damned few people in the county who didn't like James or owe him in some way. She'd totted off the exceptions and was left with a handful of names. Only one seemed useful. Melanie had been put right through to Simon Calhoun's office, trading on the Underwood name, and had spent a considerable amount of time on the phone with him. She had another appointment with him today.

Before she went to see the district attorney, she had some information to gather. Digging out her ski clothes, Melanie dressed for the slopes, because that's where she'd find the men she needed to question.

"Single!" the woman called, just before I loaded on the lift.

"Single!" I yelled back and motioned her to join me at the

front of the line. A little PR by taking a tourist up without a wait never hurt. Except this was no tourist, I realized once we'd been scooped up in the chair. This was my ultimate boss's wife, and more to the point, this was someone who'd spent far too much time with Ulf. He hadn't troubled my sleep since I spent the night with Jake and Kurt, and I didn't welcome this reminder of him. If James Underwood hadn't known what was going on in that quarter, he was probably the only one. I wished I'd kept my mouth shut at the loading zone.

"Set off any avalanches lately?" she asked brightly, once we were airborne.

"We triggered one in the back bowls of the East Peak right before Christmas." Marty and I had dragged the howitzer up with a snow cat and let fly. Shooting the gun was fun, but I'd still wondered if the echoes triggered slides on distant peaks and if someone died in the backcountry because of it, though no one had been reported missing. I dreamed three nights running after that.

"How about on Cement Chute?" she asked, and the bright-ness in her voice had gone brittle.

"Just the once, ma'am." I did *not* want to discuss that with her, of all people.

"Once was certainly enough there, wasn't it?" Mrs. Under-wood persisted. "How much did he pay you to wait?"

"No one paid me to wait for anything at all. What are you talking about?" I had a sick feeling I knew.

"You set a slide in the middle of the day," she pointed out acidly. "That's contrary to Wapiti Creek policy, and it certainly isn't safe. Now is it?"

"You're quite right, and if it had been safe to wait until the next morning, we'd have done that. But we had several people make repeated attempts to go down a closed slope those last two days, and anyone who got caught in the slide had disobeyed every warning we posted." I was angry now. "We went to trigger then in order to keep another dozen people from wandering where they could easily have gotten killed."

"Instead, you killed the one person it would have benefited my husband to have die."

"Correction, lady. I didn't kill anyone. And the only one who was trying to kill someone that day was your fuck-buddy, Ulf." Rage didn't begin to describe the white heat inside me. Only well-honed instincts to keep confrontations from escalating on the slopes allowed me to keep my voice down—I wanted to scream into her face. "I had to dig him out because he had to go where he wasn't supposed to."

"So you didn't like him. Did you kill him because you thought my husband might appreciate it?" She was snarling just as viciously as I was.

"I didn't kill him, lady." If we got to the top of the mountain without me throttling her, it would be a miracle.

"In my eyes you did, and I will never forgive you for it. Never." She spat the words out. "And when this mountain is mine, it will be my great pleasure to fire your ass, assuming it isn't rotting in prison by then."

"I have done nothing worth going to prison for, and if you think I'd stick around to work for you, you're wrong." I thought really fast about what she'd said about the mountain. "Mr. Underwood's divorcing you, isn't he?" She went white. I went silent, because anything else that came out of my mouth would get me fired for general reasons. Patrollers did not get to mouth off to the skiers, no matter how richly they deserved it. What I'd already said was probably too much, though I couldn't imagine her repeating it to my boss.

We rode the rest of the way up the hill in icy silence, and

the trip on the lift never went so slowly. Once we offloaded, I radioed my intention to patrol a blue/black slope, an advanced intermediate, because I knew her skill level. She couldn't follow me, and I probably wouldn't see her again that day. If I never saw her again, it would be too soon.

I met up with Marty toward the end of the day, about halfway down Sundance, a popular intermediate slope on the West Peak. He'd found a skier down, and I was best placed to bring the toboggan quickly. We were loading the injured man up when tiny skiers stopped to see.

"Hi, Mark!" piped Gracie, who'd become my little buddy because I hung with her pal Jake. "Hi, Marty! Whatcha doing? Aw, did you hurt yourself?" She peered into the fallen man's face. He grimaced, possibly from pain, possibly from the sting of her innocent concern.

"Honey, you keep on skiing. We're working here. See you later, okay?" I glanced up at her in time to see Jake pull up to reinforce my words.

"Gracie, we're not going to bug Mark and Marty now. You come on with me and Todd. See you tonight, guys." Jake shooed the munchkins down the hill and followed them. He must have drawn ski-nanny duty again, though as best I could tell, he really liked the kids and they certainly liked him.

Marty and I got the man loaded securely and headed downslope, Marty on the toboggan's front handles and me on the stern handle. The guy was just going to have to trust us not to spill him out on the curves as we wove down the slope, but we were good at this. He'd get to the bottom more safely in the toboggan than he'd managed on his own. Once we'd deposited him at the patrol hut and sat down with the incident reports, I had a chance to ask Marty if he'd had any interesting encounters.

"Did you run into Mrs. Underwood today?"

"You mean the trophy skank?" he asked sourly. "Oh, yeah." Soft-spoken Marty almost never used that kind of language.

"Did she accuse you of anything?"

"Plenty." Anger rolled off him. "She is so off base."

"Yeah. We'll talk about it later." I wondered how much trouble she could or would make for us, but the coroner had declared Ulf "dead by misadventure", and I thought it was a closed case. If she sought Marty out, too, she had to be on the warpath, and I didn't want to get caught in the crossfire between her and her husband. Then again, she might just be looking for a handle that didn't exist. I bent to the paperwork, eager to finish it, because I had friends coming over tonight. And Allan. That thought curved my lips and made the pen go faster.

EIGHT

The place was clean and starting to fill up; people were bringing chairs and food into my living room. I had helped Jake set up the folding table he dragged over from his place. We put it in the living room near the kitchen to hold the food, which was showing signs of being more real than not. A couple bags of chips sat toward the back of the table, but chili in a crock pot steamed next to some kind of green, grainy salad. Tabouli, Julie told me, and she was suitably impressed when I told her to leave room for the baked potatoes that could stay in the oven until we were ready to eat.

"You're more domestic already, Mark. You just needed the push." Julie popped the top off the tub of margarine and propped a bag of bacon bits next to it. Gabe came by to sniff the spread. He was as unattached as I was, and as poorly fed. Julie slapped his hand when he reached to snag a few crumbles, and they both laughed at his hurt puppy eyes.

The door was ajar and now it opened wider to let someone with a big silver pot through. "Where do I put this?" Allan asked, and I was happy to clear a spot and throw down the dish towel for a pad so he could set down his burden.

"Smells good! What is it?" I inhaled over the pot. The aroma went to the very core of my brain, prodded memories, and announced, *Home.*

"Pot roast. I heard there would be baked potatoes." He stirred the gravy a bit before turning to me with a wink. "That worked out okay?"

"Perfect. I think. They're still in the oven." I glanced around the room, which was full of people chatting. "Everyone's here except for Marty, so I should probably bring them out. I didn't want them to get cold." He snorted.

"I'll help." He followed me into the kitchen, a mirror image of his, and reached for the oven door. "Do you have a big bowl?" Chelsea buzzed through and nabbed the roll of paper towels, winking as she went by. I ignored her with dignity, instead rummaging through nearly empty cupboards for a bowl, finding only a saucepan that seemed large enough. "That will work."

Opening the oven door let a blast of steam out, which should have warned me. I grabbed a potato and dropped it much faster, muffling my yelp by sticking my hand into my mouth.

Allan winced sympathetically and pushed my hand under the cold tap. "Potatoes hold heat. You could probably insulate houses with potatoes, they hold so much heat." He turned my hand over, inspected it, and put it back into the water, never letting go of my wrist. "Everybody gets at least one potato burn." He showed me his other hand, which had an assortment of scars on it. His fingers and palm were strangely well-padded. "You're now on your way to getting 'chef's hands'."

"Great. Now I just need to cut myself a few times." He held

my wrist and the babble from the living room receded into the background.

Allan laughed. "And pick up enough hot pots that your hands try to insulate themselves." He rubbed his free thumb against another finger to show me what he meant. "But I wouldn't try for a potato barehanded even so." He grabbed a hot mitt off the counter. "Stay in the water for another minute or two." Watching him bend over the oven to flip the spuds into the saucepan was worth him letting go. I had to turn slightly sideways to disguise my reaction.

"You guys okay in here?" Kim bustled in to put some soda bottles in the fridge. "Oh, hey! Baked potatoes! Go, Mark!" She grabbed a sleeve of plastic cups and left again.

Chagrined and dried, I followed Allan and the potatoes the few steps back to the table. "Come and get it!" I called to the group. Everyone surged toward the food; most of them had spent a long day outside and were ravenous. I stepped aside, letting Kim and Devon load plates.

"Only two bags of chips and we've got eight guys here." I couldn't resist razzing Chelsea.

"Seven," she replied with a glance toward the door. "Marty's not here yet."

"What's keeping him?" It was odd that they hadn't come over together.

"He opened an envelope and said he'd be down once he called his dad." She spooned some of Allan's pot roast onto her plate and drizzled the gravy over the meat and the potato. "He sounded worried."

"Huh." Marty's father was a lawyer in Bozeman, Montana. I couldn't imagine what the matter was, and gave up trying to figure it out when I got close enough to the table to load a plate. Taking it to a bare spot on the carpet, I got waylaid by Gabe.

"Don't sit next to Julie," he whispered, and I was happy to let him have that slice of carpet. Devon was on the other side of the empty spot. I didn't want to sit next to him, not with Allan right behind me. I needed space for two, which I'd find right next to the recliner, where Kurt had planted his butt. I'd introduce him to Allan, who needed his brand of expertise on the slopes, so I left the space between me and Kurt. Too late, I noticed the magazine that had fallen from my hand the night before.

I nearly dove after it, but Allan was lowering himself to the carpet and I didn't want him to think I was grabbing his ass before we'd even eaten. Not that I wouldn't be glad to, but not with an audience. So he got a good look at a picture that I really hoped no one else had noticed. Well, no one had made a big to-do over it, so I was pretty sure it hadn't been spotted yet.

Allan, of course, noticed, since he nearly sat on it. Kurt noticed the movement and leaned over to grab the magazine. Allan just stashed it in the rack without a word, but I think he met Kurt's eyes, because Kurt dropped one eyelid in a conspiratorial wink and asked what he'd seasoned the pot roast with.

I should have done one last sweep through the apartment, but this might not work out too badly. I'd know Allan's orientation soon enough to stop thinking about someone else unavailable. The pot roast was delicious, though, and there wasn't much conversation for a few minutes, only the soft sounds of munching.

"This is wonderful!" I finally managed to get a few words out.

"Thanks," Allan returned. "It's a popular one with the

clients. I just made us an extra pan." He speared another bite of potato. "They got pot roast or white chili today."

"White chili sounds good, too." Though I wasn't sure what it was, I was quite sure it would be good if Allan made it. He was running three for three.

"It wouldn't go so well with baked potatoes. Next time, though."

That sounded even better.

The chatter ran around the room as people called out to one another about events of the day. Belatedly, I realized Allan probably didn't know anyone here. Someone across the room wondered who made the pot roast, which gave me the opportunity to fix that.

"Allan did! Guys, this is Allan Tengerdie, proprietor and chef of Almost Home Catering, who made that amazing corn chowder, too." Heads swiveled around at that. "They were ready to fight me for it," I told him, getting chuckles from everyone. "So, to your left is Kurt Carlson—see him for ski lessons—then Jake Landon, who will get you on and off the bunny lift." My voice faltered a bit, introducing those two, but I went on. "Julie Cavanaugh, ski teacher to the knee-high set. Gabe Wilson, who tends one of the expert terrain lifts." Allan wouldn't be meeting Gabe professionally this year or next, given how he wiped out on the easy slopes.

"Pay attention, there will be a quiz. Devon Parks—if you need to rent skis, see him." Devon waved. I think he was the unhappiest of us, stuck indoors all day. He'd made the cut on the ski-off last spring; he had qualified for patrol, but so had a few too many other people. Now he worked rentals just to be at Wapiti Creek, though he'd turned down a patrol slot at a different resort. "Chelsea Leindorff, also a ski instructor. Charlie Lewis is Chelsea, Julie, and Kurt's boss. If you need to know anything about anyone, see him. He's got the dirt on everyone." That provoked a wave of laughter, some rueful, some amused, and I suddenly realized that Charlie could dish the dirt on me as well as he could on anyone else. I'd have to be the one to tell my own dirt, just… not yet. "Charlie's lovely girlfriend Madison." I didn't know her well enough to add more. "Kim Brancazio you've met. She's a ski patroller when she isn't having domestic frenzies, and…." I looked around for my missing partner, who should have turned up by now. "Where's Marty?"

"I don't know. Maybe he's still talking to his dad?" Chelsea whipped out her phone. "But I didn't think he'd be this long." She dialed, spoke softly, and raised her eyebrows.

"Sounds like I've stumbled into a gathering of the royalty on the mountain," Allan commented softly. At my sideways look, he continued. "All these patrols and instructors. I'm the guy who needs the instruction."

"We ski the way you cook. Does that make you kitchen royalty?" I took another bite of meat with unfeigned pleasure.

"That's one way of looking at it." He sat up a little straighter. I hadn't flirted with anyone in a long time; Jake had shut me down before the flirting even started. Maybe I hadn't lost my touch.

Chelsea had been listening more than she'd been talking, so her voice brought other conversations down a notch when she did speak. "Okay, I'll tell Mark. And I'll bring you a plate. See you, hon." She closed the phone with a click. "Marty isn't going to join us tonight."

"Why not? Is he okay?" Concerned murmurs ran through the room, but Chelsea just gave me worried eyes and motioned to follow her into the kitchen.

"Tell me what?" I wasn't getting up—I didn't care if others heard. Chelsea sat back down.

"A process server is waiting to see if he'll be led straight to you, because he doesn't have the address. Marty doesn't plan to make it easy for him."

"Process server!" I echoed, and people swiveled to look at me. "What? Chelsea, did he say what this is about?" I didn't owe anyone any money, and I hadn't had any traffic tickets or anything at all that would account for this.

"Seems someone has decided to reopen the matter of Ulf." She sounded sick, and well she might. Marty had his own set of bad nights after watching me ski onto the slab to rescue Jake. More than anyone who hadn't been there, Chelsea knew what Ulf had cost us all in peace of mind. "I thought the coroner decided that was a death by misadventure and closed the case."

"I thought so, too." Memory tugged. "I had a nasty lift ride with Melanie Underwood today. These people won't stay out of my life. Even the dead ones."

"She sure spent enough time with Ulf," Gabe commented. "One trip to the top of the mountain per day, but I haven't seen her up top since the avalanche. What did she want?"

"She seems to think she's going to get the entire mountain and then fire my ass." This had to be tied somehow. "Chelsea, did Marty say if this is the coroner's subpoena? Or something else?" Too late, I realized that Charlie was doing everything but taking notes. He kept better track than anyone of the mountain's scandals, but having him on my side in any matter of dirt could only be a good thing. He might repeat what he'd heard, but he'd probably believe what he learned from a friend over what he heard elsewhere.

She shook her head in puzzlement. "Grand jury. Marty's dad had some advice for you. He said not to evade the process server, but you also don't have to make it easy for him. Going to work and being inaccessible in your usual course of business isn't evading. And, he said, once you get that subpoena from the grand jury, you can't talk about any of it to anyone. Not even to Marty."

"Is the process server looking for anyone else?" Jake asked. He'd risen from his cross-legged position on the floor to stand protectively over Kurt, with one hand on the back of his chair. I met their eyes, knowing who else might get legal paperwork.

"Marty didn't say, which doesn't mean anything." Chelsea set her plate on the floor in front of her and dropped her wadded napkin on it.

When we'd made our report after bringing the body down, we hadn't mentioned Jake or Kurt's names, calling them only "skier in red" and "skier in gray." If management knew they'd been on a closed ski trail, it would have cost them their season passes and probably Jake's job, since he worked directly for the resort. "The reports don't have any names in them other than Ulf's and all the patrollers who helped search, but if they ask the wrong question, I have to either answer or lie."

"Don't lie to a grand jury," Kurt advised me. "Lift tickets versus jail time, no contest. Don't do it." Jake started to say something, but Kurt overrode him. "Just don't. Any fallout from the truth will just get handled." He glanced up at Jake, who looked down with a mixture of worry and pride. Yeah, those two would handle it. I just hoped Marty and I didn't give them anything to need handling.

"Right." I set down my plate, which contained nothing that wouldn't taste like ashes now.

"Who's Ulf, and what does he have to do with my best customer?" Allan asked.

"Ulf was a ski instructor for Alpenschlössl, which you will *not* go to for ski lessons, and he was boffing Melanie, which I think Mr. Underwood is doing something about." This mountain was a damned small place sometimes, and the breeze from Charlie's flapping ears was rather strong. I saw no reason to keep Melanie's secret.

"Great." I could practically hear the calculations in Allan's head.

"He and the kids still need to eat," Jake pointed out on his way to the kitchen with his empty plate. "Hey, there's chocolate cake if anyone wants dessert." I could hear drawers open and shut in the kitchen. "Where's a knife?"

A knock on the door startled us all before I could tell him. Recalling the legal advice not to evade, I dragged myself up off the carpet to answer it. I opened it slowly and threw it wide when I recognized the familiar face on the other side of the door.

"Jorey!" I was so relieved that I nearly yelled. "Get your ass in here!" Holy crap, what was Jorey Taylor doing at my front door? "How was Austria?" I dragged him in and got that door shut behind him before any process server followed.

"It was great!" Jorey roared into my ear, pounding my back. "Good to see you, Mark, and hey, Kurt! Dude!" He let go of me to squash Kurt against his chest, and let go just as Jake came around the corner. The look on his face made me glad it was just a plastic knife in his hand. "Jake! My man!" Jorey ignored the knife, bringing a meaty paw down on Jake's shoulder.

Rooms always got thirty percent smaller when Jorey Taylor walked in, not just because he was six foot two and well over two hundred pounds. Now he was introducing himself around, because while most of us knew him, some didn't, and I could see Charlie taking mental notes. "Got another plate?" Jorey asked at last, hugging Julie in a greeting that he didn't seem inclined to end.

"Sure, let me get it." Julie squirmed out of his arms. Gabe

looked a whole lot less than happy to see the legend that used his lift, and accepted his own handshake coolly. Julie slipped behind me, letting me be the one to hand over a paper plate, which Jorey filled to an accompaniment of questions from Kim and Kurt. The mood that had gotten so somber with news of Marty and my legal woes lifted as Jorey spilled his sunlight over the room, and Gabe beamed for other reasons when Julie sat back down beside him. She slipped her arm around his, which might have been all that kept him from floating away.

From the big easy chair, Jorey held court, though I noticed that Kurt didn't sit at his feet, preferring to lean against the wall to listen after he helped Jake pass around thick slices of chocolate cake. Guess being "Jorey's Shadow" was a thing of the past.

"I won the slalom at Kitzbühel, fourth in the super combined, and second in the downhill at Schladming," Jorey told everyone while shoveling in the chow, though Kurt took over explaining about World Cup points Jorey'd earned so the latecomer could appreciate the food properly.

"We're in Loveland next week, if anyone wants tickets," Jorey put in, wiping gravy off his upper lip. "Lake Louise the week after. And I am going to marry whoever made this pot roast. Sight unseen." He looked hopefully at Kim and Chelsea.

"That would be me," Allan said dryly. He'd ended up in a folding chair during all the shifting around.

Everyone howled at Jorey, who swiveled around to see who had responded to his ill-considered proposal. Jorey was a handsome guy, less so with his jaw hanging down and his eyes slightly bugged out. He tried a quick recovery. "If your chicken paprikash is as good as this, I might have to switch teams." Everyone laughed harder except for Kurt, who shook his head and went into the kitchen for something.

And me. I wanted to punch him for making an advance, no

matter how jesting or insincere, toward Allan. Then I wanted to punch him for crushing my hopes, because Allan told him, "My chicken paprikash is better, but don't worry, I'm not interested."

Not interested. Damn. I'd have bet the other way, but he'd said it himself. Not interested. Well, as Jake had said, a guy always needs friends. The meal became a stone in my belly, though I laughed dutifully with the crowd.

"I better head home," Chelsea said, going around the table making up a plate for Marty.

A phone played a snatch of song, something my mind supplied highly suggestive lyrics for, which cut off when Jorey answered. "That was the coach," Jorey told us once he shoved his phone back in his pocket. "I'm being reeled in. Suppose I should go before he has an aneurysm. He chewed on me awhile today about being a team player, just 'cause I took off for the East Peak. Glad to see everyone, glad to meet you." He shook hands or hugged his way around the room, until he got to Allan, where he paused. "Sorry it didn't work out, darling."

"These things happen." The smile Jorey got wasn't the same as the smiles I'd gotten, letting a flicker of hope rise.

Hands laden, Chelsea paused at the door. "Who's going to go first and run interference? We don't need that guy back-tracking me here." Charlie and Madison said their goodnights and offered to distract any lurkers.

"I'll even carry that for you, babe." Jorey opened the door for her.

"Good. Take this," she said, handing him the cake and a folding chair. "My fiancé couldn't come tonight; he'll appreciate us bringing him dinner." We could hear her voice trailing off down the hall, and I had a good snort at the great Jorey Taylor striking out three times in one evening. If it could happen to him, it was a little bit easier to take when it happened to me.

The rest of the crowd milled around, clearing the food and heading out the door. Kurt snagged the cake pan. "That was pretty good. Even the cake," he razzed Jake, who took it good-naturedly.

"Told you I could, if there was a proper oven." Jake grinned at him. There had to be someone who'd grin at me like that, I thought tiredly, watching them head down the hall, laughing about how much work it was to bake a cake in a Dutch oven at their ranger cabin. I went back to the kitchen, where Julie and Allan were putting what few leftovers there were into the fridge and Kim was wiping crumbs off the folding table.

"You don't like Jorey?" Kim went into the kitchen to throw a handful of debris into the sink. "He's quite the hottie, Jules."

"Not 'like' like. He's probably got a girl in every resort. Not to mention the whores in Amsterdam." Julie snorted as she scraped the last of the tabouli into a container and handed it to Allan. I felt sorry for the guy, but if he was going to get into the newspapers—and the incident she referred to had made more than the sports section—he should expect that people would remember it. "I'd rather have someone who was actually around." She turned on the tap to rinse the bowl, and I was left with the interesting sensation of being a guest in my own home.

"I'm out of here. Think I'll go home and watch a movie." Julie wiped the bowl with a paper towel and tucked it under her arm.

"Something good?" Gabe asked, but his eyes said he'd have invited himself to watch even if it was a documentary about chickens.

"Good party, Mark." Julie kissed my cheek, and they were gone.

"Great time, Mark," Kim echoed when she collected her crock pot, and kissed my cheek as well.

"Glad you made me do it, hon." If nothing else, it was practice for doing it some more, because it was Mr. Not Interested who was wiping down counters in the kitchen. "We'll keep it up."

"Sorry we didn't get to play Twister," she said with a giggle. "I had such a good bracket system worked out, too." If she thought tossing her curls at the kitchen was supposed to cheer me, she hadn't been paying attention earlier.

"Save it for another time," I suggested.

"Oh, I will!" With a last peck she scooted out the door, first looking left and right for the process server.

"Thanks for having me over tonight." Allan shook the crumbs out of the dishtowel and hung it neatly over the oven door handle. "You have a nice bunch of friends."

"Hey, glad you could join us." I had enjoyed the fantasies while they lasted.

"Does the cleaning crew all get kissing privileges?" Allan took a step toward me.

"Huh?" Oh, that was elegant. "I heard you say you weren't interested." I wanted to take the next step toward him, but didn't.

"You heard me say I wasn't interested in Jorey Taylor, and I'm not." He tipped his face to me. "But I did like your choice of magazines."

"A guy needs something when he's unattached." I came that step closer and looked into his eyes, wondering if I'd get to lick that cleft chin tonight.

"I know. I have a few of my own." Now Allan's hands were on my waist. I put mine on his upper arms, firm with muscle that belied the stockiness in his middle.

Damn but it's fun to kiss someone half a head shorter than yourself. I leaned my head enough to meet his mouth, soft and pliant under mine, and just when I was about to part my lips and really taste him, there was a knock on the door. That deflated my growing erection and made us spring apart like guilty men.

"Fuck. The process server found me." I'd almost managed to forget about that.

"You didn't do anything awful to Ulf, did you?" Allan couldn't have heard the stories, or might not have connected them with me. Quiet suspicion filled his voice.

"No. He was in the wrong place at the wrong time, and I would have saved him if I could." There was a sick announcement in my gut that I'd dream tonight, and his face wasn't promising he'd stick around to wake me out of it. "It was just a ghastly accident."

There was more insistent rapping.

"You better get it." It had been great while it lasted, the whole one kiss of it, and now I had to let trouble in.

"Yes?" I snarled at a surprised Jake and had to apologize. "I thought you were the process server." There had been a time when I'd have liked nothing better than to have him knock on my door, but not now. "What's up?"

"Sorry. I forgot the table." Jake sheepishly entered and folded up his collapsible monstrosity. "Good night, guys." He hightailed it out of there with evidence that my life was barren and in danger of remaining so. If I actually owned a proper table, I might have had the chance to lay Allan down on it. He and I looked at each other, knowing the moment was as burst as a soap bubble.

"Good night, Mark." The kiss he put on my cheek was as chaste as Julie's or Chelsea's, and then he was just as gone.

I did dream that night, but it was Allan in the snow.

NINE

"Good morning, Charlie," James Underwood rumbled into the phone, grabbing another file off his desk. "What's happening at the ski school?"

"Nothing unusual. Classes are running around eighty percent of capacity." Charlie began his morning report. "It's what's happening off the slopes that you'll be interested in."

Underwood put everything down. "Oh?"

"Have you heard anything about a reopening of the investigation on Ulf Seiler?"

Bad ideas came floating through the phone. "No, why?"

"There's a grand jury investigation. Subpoenas are going out. The snow conditions team is spooked." Charlie was uncharacteristically serious.

Underwood made a note to call his lawyer. It didn't take too sharp a pencil to connect dots between legal trouble with Ulf's death and himself. "Charlie, how the hell do you know these things?"

"Same way I know the US Ski Team is back in town and

Jorey Taylor is on the prowl." He laughed, and then changed the subject. "Are things okay with you and Melanie?"

Underwood reflected that Charlie was never as random as he sounded. "Not something I want to discuss, Charlie. Thanks for telling me." He hung up, thinking there was more trouble on his mountain than he'd known.

The process server didn't find me on the way to work, and he certainly didn't find me as Marty and I did the dawn patrol before the lifts opened, or any time during the day. Either he wasn't working at it, or he was a terrible skier, because it shouldn't have been too hard to find me, even in a resort as big as Wapiti Creek.

I thought about the timing and the accusations. Everything about this revival of interest in Ulf screamed that Melanie Underwood was behind it. The coroner's case had been closed within days of the avalanche, and no one then had tried to make more of it than it seemed. I tried to talk with Marty about our upcoming visit to the county court, but he'd only shake his head and change the subject.

"My dad's a district attorney, Mark. I grew up on the sanctity of the law, and I'm not supposed to discuss it once I've been served."

"I haven't been served yet, so I talk, you listen," I coaxed, but he wasn't having any of it.

"Listening is half the discussion." We were on Galloping Goose, headed to the bunny slope, ready to check in with the supervisor and drop off the dawn patrol gear.

"Marty, do you really think people don't talk about stuff if it affects them, no matter what the rules are?" That got me a sour look, making me wonder if his notions would be more flexible if his father had been a criminal defense attorney. We said nothing more and split up once the lifts opened and the mountain began to fill.

The glorious Colorado blue sky held no hint of bad weather in it, and the skiers were out in droves. Wapiti Creek was never as busy as Aspen or Vail, since it was both more expensive and less accessible, but there was as big a crowd as I could recall during a non-holiday week. A good time was being had by all, making my job easy.

I did have to retrieve a couple of snowboarders from some deep powder. "I've fallen and I can't get up" is a real hazard for boarders in fluffy snow, and these two guys didn't have the sense to understand that. Champagne powder, that peculiarly Coloradan, dry, crisp snow, is a heck of a lot easier to ride if the boarder doesn't drink some champagne first. Cal hadn't understood that last season, and he didn't seem to have a better grasp of it now. He and his buddy in the Hawaiian-print pants swung between sullen and giddy when I hauled them to their feet, the whiff of alcohol on their breaths. They weren't drunk, but might be as the day went on. Cal showed no sign of recognizing me, and I was glad of it, revolted by the memories of that night. I'd enjoyed it at the time, except for the part where he compared me to his rental snowboard.

They were just another couple of young men on vacation, and just another part of my workload, I thought, watching them swoop back onto groomed snow. I'd hold out for someone who'd remember my name.

Just before lunch I arrived at the lift line again. "Single!" I advertised a shorter wait. The voice that answered warmed me even better than soup.

"Single!" Allan yelled from far back in the line, and trudged up to join me when I beckoned. "Hi, Mark! I don't usually get to skip the line when I yell that." He struggled to get both poles in one hand and still reach the mounting line.

"Stick with me, boy, you'll do all sorts of things." Maybe flirting could restore some of the mood from last night. The chairlift caught us from behind for a ride up the mountain that could either be too long or not nearly long enough.

"I was hoping for that." He glanced over at me once we were airborne. "I shouldn't have left like that."

"I can see why you did, though." I took a deep breath that did nothing for the pounding in my heart. "Maybe we should try again tonight? Without a house full of other people?" A quick mental inventory of the fridge suggested that I could offer food, even if he'd cooked the best part of the meal himself, or we might even go out. Or stay in.

"We should," he agreed. "I'll be done with deliveries and back by six. Say, six thirty? I'll bring dinner." Oh, heaven.

I was supposed to be watching the slopes to either side of the lift, but I could only look at him. "Yeah. Sounds good." Something pinged my mind—he was out skiing. "Deliveries? This isn't your day off?"

He shook his head. "I don't have a lot of those. Right now everything is in the oven and doesn't need to be stirred, so I slipped out for a couple of runs. I'll have to go back and load the van." He shifted and his hand landed on my thigh. "Do you get days off? Or is skiing just that much fun that you keep going all the time?"

"I get days off. I need the break sometimes." My hand covered his now. "After a couple of days I feel like I can't warm up. Plus there's laundry. Groceries. Life stuff. You know." Was he maneuvering me into skiing for pleasure? A novel concept for sure. I played with his hand some more, even pressing his fingers between my thighs. Not much of a leg-squeeze, because I was so lean these days, but he responded to the movement with a firm grip. "It would be fun to just, you know, ski for skiing. Not with both eyes open wide for trouble."

"It's not good to make what you love into only what you do for a living." Allan took his hand back to slide into the strap of his ski pole. "I'll enjoy watching you eat tonight." That smile would be greatly enhanced if he took the dark goggles off.

As we offloaded and I radioed in where I planned to go next, I watched him head toward the easy slopes, marked with green circles. Allan might understand the connection or divide between a passion and a need better than anyone. I could live without skiing—and maybe without cooking, since cardboard pizzas didn't count—but I couldn't go without eating. Did the food lose its savor in his mouth now and then, I wondered. If it did, would the flavor return if I fed him?

An uneventful trip down Sugar Gulch put me at the bottom of the hill in time to have lunch with some of the gang. Party leftovers made the best midday meal I'd had in a long time. I think there was a serving of pot roast left only because Gabe had been distracted by Julie, and he looked ready to fight me for it now. Lunch was a raucous retelling of the evening for Dave and the others who hadn't been there, and there were a few lifted eyebrows from Kim and Chelsea when someone suggested doing it again. I shoveled in another mouthful of leftover tabouli and wouldn't say a thing about what happened when the kitchen was clean at last. Jake had a sudden need to adjust his boot when he could have spilled the beans. I wasn't going to tell them that Allan was bringing dinner tonight. If it didn't produce another thicket of waving forks, there would surely be concerned mother-hen clucks. Fortified with good food and anticipation, I left the gang for an afternoon on the slopes.

A glance at the clock told me there was time for a hot shower, which would get the fragrance of sweaty polypropylene long underwear off. Polyprope made the warmest bottom layer, better than the microfiber polyester that I'd pretty much stopped wearing. The tradeoff for warmth was the weird rancid odor that polyprope developed by the end of the day. The smell was anti-seductive, and Allan would be here soon. I fondled myself clean but didn't go for the orgasm. I didn't want anything to take the edge of eagerness off.

If I had any insulation on me at all, I could wear layers that didn't end the day stinking. Rubbing soap over my skin, I could feel the muscles too distinctly, feel knobby bits that could leave bruises on a lover, and knew that Julie was right. I'd neglected myself. Being perpetually cold was only part of the price of not eating properly—the gaunt look might turn Allan off.

Then again, he might take plumping me up as a challenge, and that could be fun on a lot of levels. I put on a pair of jeans that used to be snug and added a belt.

Where were we going to eat? I debated running downstairs for Jake and Kurt's table and a couple of their folding chairs but didn't care to make explanations to them. Damn this bachelor existence. It had been lots of fun in the beginning, but had long since gotten old. Whereas it didn't matter before, now that I wanted to impress someone, the lack of creature comforts was achingly apparent.

Everyone had been good-natured about sitting on the floor

last night, but I wanted to do better than that. Given what I had to work with, my best idea was a picnic.

My big quilt took up most of the living room floor once I pushed the easy chair out of the way. That chair had possibilities, but not for dining. It was wide enough for two if one was straddling the other, so I stuffed a couple of things we might want later into the cushions. What else? Plates, napkins, let's see, forks go on the left, knives on the right, glasses that wouldn't tip, and I admired my handiwork. Then I brushed my teeth a third time, lest parsley from the tabouli was somehow clinging to an incisor.

Six twenty-six. Staring at the door wasn't going to make him come any sooner, and then he knocked.

TEN

Except it wasn't Allan at the door.

I stared stupidly at the middle-aged stranger holding a manila envelope who was standing on my threshold. "Mark Thomas McAvoy?"

"Yes."

He held out the envelope, and there was no point in not taking it. "You are hereby served with subpoena for the Franklin County Courts. Appear as summoned or be held in contempt."

"Your timing sucks, you know that, right?" I ripped the sealed envelope open. My stomach might have been churning, but I'd never even seen a subpoena and wanted to know what it really said.

"I looked all over the mountain for you today," he said smugly. "And I checked McTavish's for you, as well. They do a good Reuben." He turned to go, full of himself for having a nice day on municipal time.

"I know." My gaze didn't leave the paper. Where exactly did it say that I wasn't supposed to talk to anyone about any of this?

Looking up at the sound of footsteps improved the moment

considerably. There was Allan, a plastic bag dangling from his arm and a steaming pan in his hands. "He found you?"

"Yeah, and I don't see why I can't say what I want. This subpoena doesn't request silence or even say what to be quiet about." I looked back at the paper and folded it. "Unless I'm supposed to be a mind reader, I can talk about anything I want. Until I hear different." Marty's attorney father probably knew what was going on a whole lot sooner than the poor people on the other end of any subpoena. He'd have to stay silent.

"Good. I don't want you to dance around what's on your mind tonight." He headed straight to the kitchen to start a pot of water boiling. "The egg noodles should cook up fresh." Allan hunted in the most logical drawer for a big spoon and glanced approvingly at our picnic blanket. "Chicken paprikash for dinner," he said, watching me sniff the rich aromas. I wanted to hold him from behind as he cooked, but too soon for that.

Allan stirred a hefty amount of sour cream into the deep orange sauce and handed me a plate with noodles, chicken, and vegetables all swimming in the pungent liquid. I could easily gorge on such fare, but I wanted to stay lively for "dessert," so we ate with conversation, and I let Allan do most of the talking.

"Did the tourists get this today?" I twirled an orange-streaked noodle on my fork. If Jorey was around to eat with us, he might have changed teams for real.

"Yes, with some assembly required. I let them control the amount of sour cream that goes in. The ski team gets extra cartons; it doesn't harm the dish and they need the calories." He let the sauce drip off the chicken before he ate it. "So do you—you're outside all day."

"Have you ever tried to stuff in five or six thousand calories a day?" I mopped more sauce up with my next bite. "They probably feel like they're eating all the time." I actually did need that much for a while, before backing down to four thousand. Of course, I wasn't getting anywhere near that on bologna sandwiches. Allan would get the opportunity to count ribs tonight.

"I try not to do that." Allan poked himself in the middle. "But tasting for seasoning has a way of sneaking up on me."

"So Jorey wasn't pulling chicken paprikash out of thin air last night?" Damn, this was good.

"The team is a steady customer when they're here, and they trust me. They don't have much control over hotel food, and they worry about someone slipping a banned substance in." He wiped an orange streak from his lips. "Most of my customers are vacationing families who don't want to go out with small kids after a day skiing, but they don't want to cook in the condo, either."

"Little kids are adventurous enough to eat this?" The sauce had a sweet and hot bite to it.

"I do a killer mac and cheese, nothing at all like stuff from a box." That got the same disdain he'd used on canned soup—he better not look in my cupboard. "I do that and two entrées a day, though usually there are spare pans of stuff in the walk-in freezer for last-minute requests."

"Wouldn't want to turn down the business," I said, getting up for seconds.

"Tell me about patrolling." Allan eyed the last two noodles on his plate, making me think he was leaving them there as a test of willpower.

"Ski, help people, scold people, direct traffic, mark hazards." I ticked off my tasks. "Bring injured people down, fill out the paperwork. Every injury is good for an hour of desk time."

"What about avalanches?"

"That's not as much fun as it used to be." I shook my head sadly. "Watching the mountain fall away below you is one thing, but having the slab disintegrate beside you puts a whole other face on it."

"So you guys were lucky?" Allan carried our plates to the kitchen while I gathered up silverware and used napkins. "We have grapes and cheese for dessert." He laid out clusters of fruit and sliced some cheese into tiny white cubes with deft strokes of his knife.

"Very. Ulf wasn't, but he shouldn't have been there at all." I shuddered. "It still gives me nightmares." Now Allan was warned.

"I can see it. And now this legal stuff. Is that going to be a problem?" He stacked the plates in the dishwasher, which I took as my cue to put away the food.

"I don't know. It could be." Melanie Underwood's snipes about prison didn't seem so farfetched from certain angles. Marty and I had been trying to trigger the fateful slide, though the mountain had a mind of its own. I refused to think about it more tonight, because I had someone here whom I really wanted to get to know better.

He changed the subject on the way back to the quilt, carrying the little plate. "How do you even learn what to do with avalanches?"

"You went to culinary school to learn to cook, right?" He nodded. "I went to snow school. There's a refresher course through the Utah Avalanche Center every year, and my degree is in snow science." I shrugged. "People laugh, but it's a pretty vigorous curriculum. It has a heavy overlap with the engineering programs."

"I'm not laughing."

Allan's expression was serious but went to inviting when he leaned back against the easy chair with his legs extended. His thigh made my pillow; I stretched out on the quilt. This was the perfect way to eat dessert, I thought, accepting the morsel of cheese he popped into my mouth. I was certainly willing to be seduced, and he accepted the grape from my fingers. The cheese he wouldn't open his lips for, so I ate it and offered another grape from the plate balanced on my chest. Allan let me slip the little fruit between his lips and nibbled gently at my fingertips, a favor I returned as he fed me.

I didn't think either one of us could prolong this until all the grapes were gone. He had one hand in my hair, smoothing down the long, fine strands, and now I had the other in my mouth, because I was tired of fruit and wanted him. His arousal was as plain as mine and growing from the way I sucked his fingers; both his face and his groin, just inches from my eyes, telegraphed what he thought of my tongue dancing over his fingertips. I made that last as long as I could before turning my face against him, to worry gently at his fly with my teeth and feel his erection trying to escape through the jeans.

Then I was up to claim his mouth, pulling off his sweater, tugging his jeans away, raising my arms to let him strip me. Oh, he was warm—I pulled him down to the quilt, our skins together, mouths frantic, hands demanding. He filled my arms and overwhelmed my senses with the taste of his skin, letting me inhale tangy, paprika-scented man and pull the heat from his body. His breath was hot on my shoulder where he nuzzled me, searching out more places to lick, and his cock ground against my hip when he rolled on top of me. I wanted him desperately, and as I plunged my tongue back into his mouth, I wondered vaguely how I'd managed to finish dinner first.

Allan met me thrust for thrust with mouth and hips, his hands shoved under me to pull me close, making it easy to grab his ass. Warm, he was so warm. The soft layer of padding over his torso only meant that he had heat to share with me and something to hold on to. Handholds on me were sort of bony, but I lifted my hips for him to grab my butt and let him roll us until I was on top, pumping against his thigh and moaning into his mouth.

"How much do we want tonight?" I pulled back enough to ask.

"How much are we prepared for?" Allan gasped, sticking his finger into my crack.

"Everything." If I could dig it out of the cushions, because that meant letting go of him.

"Then let's just see how it goes." Allan kissed me fiercely again and wiggled his finger, making me moan and laugh into his mouth, and rolled us over once more.

"Yow!" I pushed back the other way and groped behind me. Allan lay on his back, eyes wide.

"Did I hurt you?"

"No." I found the fork that had just stabbed me in the butt and showed it to him.

"Think that's a sign for us to slow down?" He rolled to his side and started to stroke my back.

"Just a sign I'm a slob." I tossed it toward the kitchen, where it clattered on the linoleum. "Where were we?" Off and rolling, and it ended with him hovering over my groin, with my cock in his hand and a perplexed look.

"Protection?" He could keep pumping me like that, but yeah, I wanted his mouth on me so I sat up, kissing him for strength, and produced a square packet from the chair cushions.

"Sit." He plopped me into that big chair and knelt between my knees, ripping the foil carefully. Using his lips to unroll the condom over my cock, he shielded us from our pasts and wrapped his tongue around me. I'd let him do that as long as he liked, and he liked, oh he liked, sucking me into that warm, warm mouth. His hair was coarse and wiry under my hands, and it lay close to his scalp in dark waves, so tempting to yank when the orgasm tightened my balls and rolled through me. Allan rested his face against my belly while I recovered, holding my deflating cock until he could make a quick trip to dispose of the condom.

When he returned, he treated me to a good look at his body, and it was fine indeed. His cock stood tall and proud from bare skin—he must manscape heavily. His arms were strong and his chest broad. If a little too much of his good cooking padded his frame, I didn't care; I just wanted to wrap my arms around him. He knelt again, this time with his knees on either side of my thighs, so I could put my face to his skin and be held close.

"What do you want me to do for you?" I murmured, groping his ass with the hand that wasn't pulling him tight.

He groaned. "Mark, I have been watching you put things in your mouth all night that weren't me. I can't stand it anymore." He leaned down to kiss me and I licked the little cleft in his chin, which was as smooth as his chest. "Those lips were made to kiss." He did, pulling my lower lip into his mouth and tonguing it. "And they were made to suck a man until he screams." He thrust his tongue into my mouth again and then whispered, "Make me scream."

More than one condom lurked in the cracks of the chair. I tipped him backward onto the quilt until I lay on top of him. "Like the wide mouth?" I asked seductively, to tease him and because I wanted to hear him say that he liked my oddest feature.

"Hell, yes, Mark. I want to be in that wide mouth." His hips bucked against me, but I held him pinned. "Please." Still, he didn't complain when I kissed him deeply again before getting up enough to sheathe him.

Long and curved, his cock pointed toward his belly, but I held him upright before slipping my lips across his shaft. Teasing him, lipping him, licking him, but never quite taking him into my mouth, I played with his beautiful cock until he rose up on his elbows to beg. "Please, Mark, suck me now!" And I did.

I wrapped my generous mouth around him, giving him lips and tongue until his elbows went out from under him. His shaft glided in and out of my mouth, bringing soft moans and little cries, and he clenched his hands into the quilt, his knuckles whitening. He didn't rip the quilt when he came, though he screamed as he pumped the condom full of semen, giving me, and yet not giving me, that precious mouthful. I let him come down off the orgasm before making my own trip to the trashcan, and then wrapped us up in the quilt, which gapped a little on top of us.

"Wow, that was good." Allan burrowed his face into my neck.

"Yeah. Even with the condoms." I would rather have felt mouths against bare skin, but safety first.

"Damn, but I hate the taste of latex. Though the strawberry flavor helped," he hastened to add. I knew what he meant. It was still strawberry latex.

"Have a grape." I groped behind me and found the little plate. One grape I offered to Allan between my lips. He took it with a kiss. The other I ate, using the juices to rinse my mouth, and the next kiss was barely latex at all. "Stay tonight?"

"My pleasure," he purred, and we got up off the floor. Once in the bed, I wrapped up tight against his back, under the quilt that had gone back to its proper place.

"Think we can do oral without the condoms? Safely?" Damn, this was an awkward topic—I had no idea how to go about this except straight out.

"I'm good, can show you the paperwork tomorrow." He yawned before going on. "I test regularly, just because I'm in food service and don't want any uncertainty, not that there's a transmission issue. You?"

"Clear, as of three weeks ago." I didn't want to tell him that it was my third test since last April. The physical risks of the life I'd been living had dawned on me early on, turning me into a "no glove, no love" man, but I didn't fool myself about being safe. Too many old friends were swallowing too many expensive pills for the illusion to persist. Celibacy had damned few charms but no viral transmission was one of them. "I don't think that will change. My social life has been pretty quiet."

"I know."

That one soft comment brought my head right off the pillow. "You do? How?"

"You used to be seen at the Moose Rack Brewery, the Winged Wolf, and Tatterdemalions with clockwork regularity. Then you dropped off the map. Except for once a week at McTavish's, which isn't exactly a party spot." He drew fingertips down my forearm. "Restaurant staff talk, Mark, and we all know each other. I used to cook for Winged Wolf before I went independent."

He knew, and he didn't even have to talk to Charlie. "I wondered why the food went downhill. Must have been after you left." Then he must be able to fill in the blanks about me, because I was never there with the same person twice. I hadn't been at any of them since the lifts closed last spring.

"Probably. I had my own wild days, but I started wanting

something different out of life." Allan's fingers quit stroking and just pressed flat against my arm. "What changed for you?"

"Wanting something different out of life sounds about right." A relationship with some longevity, for one. Some respect. Someone watching my back, and I'd watch his. I thought I had all that once, but I'd been proven wrong. After him, I took what I could get, from whoever would give it to me. None of that got said aloud. I think he heard it anyway.

"I'll treat you better than they did." Allan craned over his shoulder to catch my eye, then lay back down, scooting closer to me. "You deserve it."

I did deserve better, and had high hopes I'd found it. Finally I relaxed enough to sleep, wrapped around my new teddy bear.

ELEVEN

The scent of bacon teased me awake, bringing me to a sudden awareness that Allan was still here. This morning I felt entitled to hold him from behind and match his steps through the kitchen, watching him assemble a hot breakfast, which he built into a perfectly decadent creation captured in toast.

I don't think it was just cupboard love that had me watching him cook, loving the idea of Allan doing his brand of magic for me and in my home. He brought warmth, life, and good smells into my world, and I suddenly wanted to keep him forever. I'd buy him any size skillet he wanted if he'd stay.

"This will keep you warm on the slopes." He turned in my arms and handed me a plate. We repaired to the big chair to eat, and the meal had extra savor because of Allan sprawled partially across my lap.

His own breakfast was less lavish than what he created for me. He'd put all of the bacon on mine, and added no butter or mayonnaise to the lone piece of toast that cradled his single egg. I said nothing, knowing he'd be near food most of the day, but I did feed him a sliver of bacon from my lips as a tasty caress. He licked the flavor from my mouth, reminding me of last night and kindling a huge need to take him back to bed for naked calisthenics.

"You touched me in the night," I semi-remembered. "Was I good to you? Can I do it some more now?"

Allan chuckled. "I wasn't sure you were quite awake. You were thrashing around, but you got quieter."

Before I got temporarily noisier, probably. "I don't remember dreaming, I think." The memories were misty.

"A nightmare about the avalanche?" He'd been listening last night.

"Yeah. I'm glad you interrupted it." I'd rather talk about what I'd do to him next. Strawberry condoms didn't have to be tasted.

"Glad to." Allan looked at his watch. "I would love to stay and roll around with you, but the food truck is going to pull up at my door in twenty-five minutes, and I want us to take our time. Tonight?" He gave me hopeful brown eyes.

"Tonight. Here or your place?"

"Here. My bed is a fold-out couch in the living room. Randi does not need to walk in on us, and besides, the place reeks from her cigarettes." He made a face.

"Tonight, then." With a last kiss he was gone, leaving me with a greasy pan, a full stomach, and a goofy smile.

"Single!" I yelled at the base of the lift, ready to go up the mountain for the third time that morning.

"Single!" came back in a grim voice, and Melanie Underwood was suddenly next to me again. "We need to talk."

"No, we don't. Single!" I shouted again.

"Get on the lift, guys!" the operator said. "Don't keep everyone waiting."

Keeping my temper was the highest priority, although I could probably find a few places to stash the body if I did strangle her. Eyes to the slopes, I refused to acknowledge that she rode next to me. It didn't faze her in the least.

"Get anything interesting lately?" she prodded. I didn't answer, so she asked again. "Get anything interesting?"

"I got laid. How about you?" No sooner were the words out of my mouth than I was ashamed for using what Allan and I had as a weapon against her.

"Anything on paper?" Her voice had a nasty edge.

"Old news is all. Nothing to be concerned about." Remaining calm was taking a toll on me.

"That's what you think. You know damned well what it's about, and why you should be concerned."

"Really? Why?" I would not be the one to lose my temper this time.

"Because if you play it right, you could be a very wealthy, very happy man." Mrs. Underwood's voice had gone from harpy-shrill to low and enticing. I did look at her now.

"I have nothing to play." We had way too much mountain to ascend still; I wanted off this lift right now.

She put her hand on my arm. "Of course you do, dear. Just tell them *all* the instructions my husband gave you, and you could go from ski patrol to boss, with so *very* many perks."

I yanked my arm away. "All of which I could enjoy right after I finish a twenty-five-to-life sentence for a murder I didn't commit?" Either this woman was the bluntest crayon in the box, or she thought I was. "I have no intention of lying to a grand jury, lady, and any story you want told about your husband is going to be a lie. Did you even consider that it would drag me down with him? There is nothing you can offer that would change that."

She looked so crushed it was like I'd kicked her puppy. Comical, if she hadn't been bringing up ways to incriminate myself falsely. Maybe men had been stupid for her before, but I wouldn't be one of them.

"I didn't say it was your fault, just that there were instructions you didn't think of so much at the time, which made conditions right for such a 'tragic accident'." She put her hand on my thigh and blinked up at me. I didn't appreciate any of that as a rescue-her-stupid-plot tactic; my thigh was Allan's territory. I put her hand back in her own lap rather firmly.

"Dream on."

"Think about it, because the alternative could be so much worse." As a comeback, that was really lame, because the alternative was tell the truth and everyone walk away happy. Except her. Too bad. I refused to say another word for the rest of the ride up the mountain. Although my peace of mind was now tattered, because so many odd things had indeed happened that day.

We offloaded at the top, letting me get away from Mrs. Underwood at last. Finding an out-of-the-way spot at the edge of the loading zone to radio in let me watch which way she went, so I could be certain to go some other way. Then I did a double take.

"Hello, Mrs. Underwood. Having a good day?"

I didn't expect to hear his voice again until tonight.

I must have just missed Allan getting on the lift, and now he was talking pleasantly to the poisonous bitch.

"Not especially, Allan. I think I'll head home once I finish this run. Oh, can you do single portions? I find my... needs have changed." She looked at her watch. "I would have put the request through the website, but it still isn't working right."

"I know. I can either cook dinner or stop and learn some html, because I'm not getting both done," Allan replied ruefully. "I haven't found a designer I can afford."

"Too bad, dear. I need to do a change of address, too, but I'll leave that as a voice mail." She smiled at him, but it wasn't friendly.

"Oh. So that's instead of the dinners to the main house? Or in addition to them?" Allan's voice hadn't changed. Had he spotted the venom? I hung back, waiting for them to finish the conversation.

"Instead of. Just credit back the prepaid plan, and we'll stretch this out over more meals, all right, darling?" She patted his arm and took off with a wave before he could say any more. I was there at his side before he started down the hill.

"Allan! Hey!"

He turned that blinding smile to my voice, and my heart jumped a little. Damn, but I thought I was falling in love this morning, and I was sure of it now. "Hey, Mark!"

"Leaving things in the oven again to bake?" I teased him.

"Yeah, thought I'd get a few runs in before I had to go load and deliver. How's the day going?" He pointed down the hill, and we slid that way as we talked. I could match him turn for turn and stay in speaking distance, no problem.

"Not too bad, except for that last ride up the ski lift. Hey, Allan, check with Mr. Underwood before you make any big changes to their meal plan."

He turned and almost overbalanced, but stayed on his feet. Once he regained his bearings, he asked, "Why?"

"Because she's the one I rode with, and she's trying to do her husband some dirt. So check with him first." Vindictive woman, and now she was angry with me. There probably wasn't much she could do, though.

"Good idea. I will—whoah!" His last turn took him farther than he meant to go. He ended on his side, head pointed downhill.

I pulled up below him and sidestepped up. "You okay?" He took my offered hand and pulled himself up in one smooth motion.

"Yeah. Just wounded pride." Allan shrugged and poled into motion again.

"Keep going!" I called, because off to one side of the slope were a couple of people who looked like they were about to come to blows. The screaming carried and the body language promised violence, so of course I had to ski over and intervene. No brawling on Wapiti Creek's terrain.

"Hello, all," I said pleasantly as I arrived at the side of the slope. Sometimes just by showing up and speaking, a patrol could defuse a situation. "Good snow conditions today, don't you think?"

"Terrific." Irony-laden, the word was nearly spat at me, and the man glared back at the woman.

"Yeah, fine." She was equally furious.

"Great. Tell you what, how about one of you take a head start, and the other wait here with me for a few minutes, and we can all go back to enjoying the snow?" Separate the combatants, first priority. They'd recognized the burgundy jacket and what it implied, because they had turned on me as if they'd take me out before going back to savaging each other with words or otherwise. Discretion won out, and neither lit into me.

"Fine. I'm outta here anyway." The man aimed downhill and took off with a moderate amount of skill, enough for the green easy run, turning slightly to keep the speed down. I waited until he gained some distance before turning to her.

"When you catch up to each other again, it probably won't be so bad." Or it wouldn't be on the slopes where other people could get dragged into their disagreement, willy-nilly.

"Maybe. Are we done here?" The gimlet gleam in her eye promised that the fight wasn't over yet, but he had a head start.

"You tell me. Are we done?" With only one, I didn't have to pretend that things were normal.

"We are." She gathered herself to take off. "But I am sure as hell not done with him."

She was a much better skier than her companion, and was down the hill in a cobalt blue streak, aiming for his retreating back. Catching up fast, she blew by him like a rocket; he wobbled in her passing. I took off after her, intending to pull her over and settle her before she knocked someone over or scared them down, but I was too damned slow.

Allan lay sprawled in the snow.

TWELVE

I was on the radio almost faster than I could get down the hill. This had already escalated to the point where I could ground her for reckless skiing, but I couldn't chase her. Allan needed me.

"Woman about age thirty, in cobalt blue matching pants and jacket, red-and-white K-2 skis, name engraved, all I caught was 'S-H' skiing recklessly down Park Place, headed toward the base of the Lower Scott lift. Catch her and hold her, because I may need a stretcher for her victim." I shoved the radio back in my pocket and knelt next to Allan, who hadn't tried to get up. Bad sign.

"What hurts? Anything?" I had to assess his injuries, but I hoped he was just winded from the fall. His grimace said that was wishful thinking.

"Arm. Left wrist. Great." He tried moving his legs to bring his skis parallel, but stopped. "Right leg."

"Did you hit your head on anything? Did you pass out at all?" The questions were protocol, not something I expected him to answer positively to.

"I whacked my forehead on my pole on the way down. Somebody went by real fast, and I went over. They didn't even run into me." He sounded disgusted.

"I saw. Damn, you're bleeding." I took my glove off and pushed his hair out of the way to examine the pressure cut. "Double vision? Can you wiggle your toes?" I went on with the assessment, and we established that he wasn't getting down this mountain on his own power. I dragged the radio out of my pocket again. "We need a toboggan here." Not knowing how long that might take, I removed our skis and stuck them in Xs just above him, to warn other skiers away. Getting run over too wouldn't improve Allan's situation at all. I helped him straighten out from his semipretzel state once we determined his back wasn't injured. "Did you have these scratches on your skis before?"

"No. Looks like she went right over the backs of them. This sucks." Allan craned over to look, then flopped back on the snow.

"I know. But I'll get you down the hill, and we'll see how bad it is." One of my hands rested on his arm, but I wanted to gather him up and tell him everything would be all right.

"I need to get back to the kitchen. There's stuff that needs stirring, and then packing and delivering." It wasn't getting done by him, not the way he winced when he'd tried to take his glove off.

"Who can you call? You aren't going anywhere except to the ER."

He looked alarmed. "I can't afford the ER! Not the bucks, not the time. Shit."

"Allan, if you were going to ski away under your own power, you'd have done it by now. You're hurt." I caressed his face and glanced up the hill to see Kim coming toward us with the toboggan.

"Oh no! Allan!" She met his gaze before he turned away.

"Hi, Kim. Wasn't planning on seeing you professionally." His face went red again but we all pretended it was from the cold.

Kim and I splinted his arm and his leg, and I tried to see him as one more casualty on the slopes, but I couldn't. In helping, we hurt him, and it twisted my gut to hear him hissing through his teeth. Once we had him splinted, he was able to assist us with getting on the toboggan.

"See, you're moving yourself. That's good." I wanted to be reassuring, but we both knew it wasn't going to get him out of an ambulance ride. The trip down the hill, Kim steering in front, me stabilizing in the rear, was the second worst transport I'd done. At least Allan was breathing.

Shifting him to the gurney put his face in kissing range, but the ambulance driver was tapping his foot, ready to take off. "I'll see you tonight, Allan. It will be okay." There were several things I could think of that were so not okay here, and Allan had either thought of them, too, or would. Squeezing his hand had to suffice for now, but I'd be with him later. I'd take care of him.

The woman in cobalt was sitting at a bench in the patrol hut. I motioned her to sit by my desk while I worked on the case she caused. Face like storm clouds, she put together why I had her sitting there listening to me call the hospital and give the particulars to the ER doctor. This was a conversation I had every few days, but today I ended the briefing with, "Take real good care of him, Doc." By the end of that call, she lost the attitude and looked chastened.

I set the phone down and turned to her. "You know why

we're here?" She nodded. "I just put a good man in an ambulance because of you." She hunched up tighter. "He runs a small business, and if he's hurt badly enough he can't work for a while, he may lose it. All because he was in your way."

"I didn't mean to get that close."

"You ran over the tails of his skis and brought him down. He's got grounds to sue." I let her think about that a minute, then handed her a business card from the hospital. The patrollers kept stacks of them in our desks. "Do the right thing." The mountain of paper on the incident wasn't going to get smaller for waiting, but I listened and wrote as she called and offered a credit card number. One less thing for Allan to worry about, though I couldn't do anything about what was bubbling in his pans.

I let her go, though her lift ticket stayed in the patrol hut. When I went back to the slopes, it was with a heavy heart, because I had no way to find out about Allan until I arrived at his doorstep.

THIRTEEN

The hours before closing dragged on and on, and it was with great relief that I did my final sweeps for strays. The shuttle ride back to the apartment took at least a month, because I wanted to go pelting up the steps to apartment 345 and find Allan.

I nearly went past the couple on the stairs before I realized I'd found him. A small woman in jeans and a parka had her arm around his waist and was trying to help Allan up the stairs; they'd gotten partway up to the second floor. The steps from the street level to the front door took them who knew how long, and I watched in horror as they tried to get him up a step. One ankle was braced and he wasn't touching it down at all. His weight had to be all on her shoulders, and when I got level with them, I could see that the arm over her shoulder had a brace as well. My heart sank.

"Allan!" He turned to my voice and that brilliant smile gave me the first hopeful feeling I'd had since he fell. "Let me help you here, okay?"

"Yes, please," puffed his assistant, helping Allan transfer his weight to my shoulders. "We aren't doing so good."

"You were doing real good, Penny." Allan looked gratefully at her. "We got this far."

"I'll do better to get back in the van and get the chow delivered. It's late as it is. Call me, okay?" Penny didn't stop to be introduced, and if there was hot food to be delivered, I wouldn't hold up his only ally. I listened to her retreating footsteps and dared to kiss him hello.

"Good arm around my neck, Allan, and that will put the damaged leg against me. It will be easier to get upstairs that way." And that would have worked, too, except that he was already so tired. By the time we got to the second floor landing, the breather he got when I turned up had already worn off. He leaned heavily against me.

"Mark, I don't know if I can keep going…."

But he didn't have to—I picked him up. One arm behind his back, one under his knees, a heave-ho, and off we went. Now, I would like to claim that—being the excellent physical specimen that I am, all whipcord muscle and sinew—I marched up those stairs singing, but the fact is that Allan outweighed me by probably twenty-five pounds and I'd been skiing hard all day. By the time we got to the third floor, I was panting and more than a little worried that I'd drop him just because his ski clothes were both slippery and shifting around, so I set him down gently. "Get your keys out." Then I threw him over my shoulder and got him the rest of the way to his door, unlocked it, and brought him in. Depositing him on the couch got a sigh of relief out of both of us.

"Hiya." I gave him a better greeting now, one with a big kiss. Then I peeled him down to his long johns and inspected the damage. Calling the ER had gotten me no information at all. Damn that patient confidentiality crap: I was worried. "Tell me what's what, Allan."

"Damaged ligaments in the wrist and ankle. The cut on my forehead you already know about." Allan sagged against me, letting me cuddle him. "No weight bearing on the ankle for two days, and the arm…well, the same. And then limited use, weight bearing as I can tolerate it, and the braces stay on for a while. Mark, how am I going to cook?"

I wanted to say *What's the problem?* until I imagined how heavy a pan with food for seventy-five, or three pans with food for twenty-five, might be. "We'll come up with something. Who's Penny?"

"My part-time employee. She cleans hotel rooms early in the day and then drives deliveries with me in the afternoon. She can't do it all."

"We'll work on this. Did you get lunch?" Time to do something about things I could really fix.

"No."

Great. He'd had a decent breakfast, but that was many hours ago. "I'll make you some dinner." Think fast, think fast…

He groaned. "The appetizer should be a pain pill. That last one is about worn off, but there's a bottle in my jacket pocket."

The bottle contained something that would either really help or knock him for a loop. "Is this what they gave you earlier?" He nodded.

"It works pretty good." He watched with hooded eyes as I opened the bottle and brought some water. I popped it in his mouth and both of us tipped the glass to his mouth. "Thanks. There's corn chowder in the fridge still, maybe heat some of that?"

Not only did he not have to risk my lack of culinary skills, I didn't have to demonstrate them. While the chowder heated, I peeled off my outerwear, leaving jacket, bibs, and several pairs of socks in a pile by the door. I sat back down next to him in nothing but long johns and pulled him against my shoulder. I would have fed him, but he had a good right hand to run the spoon, so I held him and the bowl of soup, contenting myself with occasionally nuzzling him. Before the first spoonful touched his lips, he paused.

"Something's off about it; it smells odd."

"The odd smell is me," I confessed glumly. "The polyprope underwear gets funky by the end of the day, but it's warm."

He took a deep whiff of me. "Hmm. Once you hit the shower, you can wear something of mine." Would anything of his stay on my hips? It didn't matter, since naked with Allan was my preferred state. "My sweatpants will cover you, if not exactly fit you." Naked maybe wasn't what he needed right now. "They're in that box."

The box he pointed at was one of several stacked against the wall with the open sides out, making a rack of shelves of a sort. A dresser stood in the corner, old oak with a mirror that tilted. Odd for a living room, but this was a one-bedroom apartment and he certainly wasn't sharing intimate space with the elusive Randi. I wondered when she'd be back.

"Food first, if you can stand me."

"I can stand you." He nestled against me and ate the chowder slowly, as if the spoon was heavy. "You plan to have some?"

"After you've had all you want." I hugged him with both arms once the dish was empty, and when I came back to the couch with a bowl for myself, he held it for me so I could keep my hold on him.

"Good stuff." I nibbled his ear softly.

"Into the shower, stinky boy."

As pet names went, I hoped that one didn't stick, and dutifully rummaged in the box.

"There's something you need to read at the bottom of the second stack, under the polo shirts."

Paper crackled under the fabric. I pulled out a single sheet with a laboratory's header. The results on it matched what he'd said. I love a man who tells me the truth. I grinned at him—he flashed me a wink. I put it back among the clothing and rummaged for something that fit.

Black sweats with elastic ankles would work. The drawstring would probably keep them from falling. I took that and a T-shirt into the bathroom, leaving my poor hurt guy leaning back with his eyes shut. Once the polypropylene scent was scrubbed off, I came back to a man who might have been asleep.

I tipped him over gently, thinking I'd find a blanket to throw over him, but he was awake after all.

"The absence of pain is pleasure," Allan told me. "The pill is kicking in."

"Good." I knelt by the couch to kiss him. "Does this thing fold out?"

"Yes. But I'd really like a shower first. Oh, damn. No shower, can't get these splint things wet." He raised his arm to glare at the Velcro-fastened brace that covered his palm and forearm. "And I can't take them off tonight."

"I'll draw you a bath." I had noticed that his tub wasn't at all scary like mine used to be.

The water ran hot as I helped him into the bathroom and sat him down to finish undressing him. A couple of shifts and pivots got one foot into the tub, and then he held onto me to lower into the water, the braced leg propped on the edge and the braced arm sticking upright. He sighed at the warmth of the little waves slapping over his skin and then gave the shampoo bottle a sour look for being far above his reach in the wire rack. He didn't have to worry; I'd take care of him.

The blood from the pressure cut had been cleaned off his face at the ER, but there was still a bit in his hair, so I dampened it with water poured from a cup stolen from the sink. The dark waves lying close to his scalp barely changed with the wetting, and then disappeared into the white lather I rubbed into being from the shampoo. Allan lay back and let me wash his hair, a job that needed lips brushed over his face. "This is decadent," he murmured into my mouth. Good. He needed some pleasure after today.

The soap made white swirls of suds over his skin. I turned my attention to his body, running slick hands over him, massaging. "What happened to your body hair?" He was really smooth, with only short tufts in his armpits and nothing at his groin, which I'd made the most of last night while mouthing him.

"It gets hot enough in the kitchen like this. It's worse with a fur coat on, so I manscape. Like it?" With his good hand he slid my hand across his chest.

"Oh yeah." I went slowly, enjoying how he looked, partly submerged and soapy, his eyes closed and a contented look that quirked into a smile. I ran my hands up and down his torso again. He was at half-mast, making me wonder what, if anything, he'd be up for tonight. All he had to do was lie back, though—I'd do all the work.

His legs first, though; one getting soap all the way to the toes, the other to the knee. Then at last to his groin, which would be so damned clean once I took care of him....

Allan grew under my hands as I stroked the suds over his flesh, into the crevices, and over the bulges, exploring more than washing, and he moaned. Bending his good leg let me have access to his taint and his crack, which were as smooth as the rest of him; I checked with soapy fingers along the crevice.

Little circular motions around his hole brought more sounds from him and lifted his hips to thrust into my grip. Getting him washed was certainly a two-handed affair.

Man, but I loved to look at him writhing under my hands, and small sounds escaped me, too. Hard as a rock myself, with no underwear to bind, I pushed against the side of the tub. Not good enough: I wanted to press against Allan.

"Not here, Mark!" he gasped and grabbed my wrist. Damn, he was strong. "I have to touch you back. Couch."

"Wait here." Unnecessary words; he wasn't getting out of the tub without help, but I said it anyway, bolting out to unfold our landing pad. The sheets and blanket had been folded up with the mattress, so all I had to do was yank the whole thing out and level before returning to lift him from the water. Now I could help him balance on one foot, leaving a wet body print on my clothing. The towel drank up the water when I hugged him dry, though I buried my face into the moist skin at his neck and licked the water away. I wanted him so bad, and damn, he wanted me, too.

Allan was dry enough, or drying as foreplay was done. "Hup!" I heaved him into the air, and he wrapped his legs around my waist. Getting through the door took some wiggling, but then I had only a few steps to the couch, where I managed to drop him on his back in a semi-controlled fashion. Of course, I fell with him and our mouths were together before the springs stopped squeaking.

If the sweatpants weren't in the way, my cock would be knocking at his back door, and his erection pressed against my belly. I let go just long enough to pull everything off and then was back on top of him, held tightly. "Am I hurting you?" I managed to ask, rubbing my length against his crack. "I don't want to hurt you."

"That's what the lube is for, Mark," he stopped nipping my neck long enough to point out. "Condoms and stuff in the side table drawer."

I'd meant his arm and leg, but if he wanted to skip right past those, fine. I tried rummaging with one hand and not letting go, but had to get up enough to find what we needed. He watched with hungry eyes as I rolled the latex over my cock and squished a glob of lube on. Another glob was for him—I put slippery fingers to his hole and went on where I'd left off in the tub, swirling and then entering, slicking him to the sounds pulled from deep in his throat.

The brace was rough on my shoulder where Allan propped his injured leg on me; his good leg curled around my waist. "Fuck me, Mark," he begged, and I didn't have to be asked twice. Slowly, slowly, I pushed in, letting his body adjust around me, and that first penetration was exquisitely tight. Once the head had breached his ring of muscle, I stopped, afraid to go on and yet desperate to plunge the rest of the way. "Ease into me, Mark, come on in," he coaxed and pulled me forward with his leg. "Yeah, Mark, ohhh…."

Oh, yeah…. Little slow strokes grew longer but not faster, not only to let me keep control, last as long as I could. I had to avoid bumping him, jostling him around, making him remember he was hurt; I had to let him feel as good as I could make him feel. We held each other's hands, letting me brace against him to fuck him slowly, and I would have leaned against him more, felt his strength, had I not also felt the Velcro and straps against my palm. If I took that hand away and wrapped it around his cock, that would make things even better, so after leaning down for a long, tonguing kiss, I stroked him, trying to match the speed of my hand and my hips.

Allan cried out from my thrusts. Happy noises, not mixed

with pain, I thought anxiously. He threw his head back, eyes closed, and pulled me against him with his leg, urging me faster. He was open to my body, open to my sight, and the wonder of it soon fountained into my orgasm, freezing me against him as the exquisite shudders rolled over me. Good, oh, man, so good, but I'd stopped moving my hand, too, and Allan wasn't done yet, though I think he'd been close.

"Let me take care of you now," I mumbled, kneeling lower between his legs. I looked up at him with his hard shaft in my mouth, watching him watch me suck and stroke him. His eyes were hooded with pleasure and not pain this time. He leaned up on his good elbow and stroked my hair with the braced hand. The Velcro caught my hair, so he stopped, letting me do all the moving. Yeah, oh good, yeah, he was close, I could tell, and then he pulsed and spurted thick come down my throat. Tonight it was mine, and I drank him down, loving the salt and the proof that I'd taken good care of him. With my face against his belly, I held him in my mouth as he went soft, stroking a little with my tongue now and then just to feel his shivers. I shivered, too, but because my exposed hind end was cold.

He put his arms out to me, inviting me to join him under the covers, which I did once I placed ice packs on his injuries and doused the light. It was still very early, but I sank into the blankets and pulled him against my chest, carefully keeping my hands and feet away from the chill at his wrist and ankle.

"Good thing Randi didn't walk in on us." Maybe she had— I'd been so engrossed in him a brass band might have marched through.

"She won't be home until well after midnight, but yeah." He laughed.

"Think you can sleep?"

"Think I have to. That pill kicked in a bit more." Allan

cuddled tighter, his braced forearm lying on my chest, and his breathing soon became soft and regular. I would have dozed off, too, but nagging thoughts kept me awake. The clock on the table blinked as the number changed to 7:17. We'd gotten through today, but what was Allan going to do about tomorrow? He'd have been fretting about it if he hadn't been full of pain pills, I was sure, so I'd fix it before he had the chance to fret. He didn't wake when I slithered out from under him and pulled the borrowed clothing back on. My keys were in my bib pocket, and I left my apartment door open once I'd dropped everything on the bed and went around the building pounding on doors.

"My place, ten minutes!" I hollered, not bothering to see who opened. "Meeting! We have a problem!"

FOURTEEN

I thumped on all my friends' doors, and a few that belonged to people Allan liked well enough to feed cinnamon rolls, so maybe they'd want to get in on the act. "Apartment 310!" I clarified for them, and in a few short minutes, my living room was packed with people.

"What's wrong?" Kim asked. I waved a few more people in and waited to explain once the room was full.

"Okay, everyone, here's the deal. Everyone here knows Allan Tengerdie, right?" That brought murmurs of agreement with a few puzzled questions. "He got hurt today, and he needs our help. Some tourist ran him over, and now he's got injuries to his ankle and wrist. So he's having a hell of a time getting around, and he's going to need help from all of us."

"I have a pair of crutches. Does he need them?" That was from one of the cinnamon roll friends, someone I didn't know.

"Yes, he does." I was going to make a drugstore run, since carrying him around until he healed wasn't happening, but this was way better. She scurried out the door, solving one more problem.

"The other big problem is that he can't cook one-handed, and he can't put Almost Home on hold until he's better. So, we need to help." That got another round of murmuring. "Our days off aren't all the same, right?" I'd given this some thought, both as to what Allan needed and what would get him that help. "The way his day works is he's in the kitchen all morning, and then he gets out and skis in the afternoon, then does deliveries. If we all give him a morning or two, everything gets done and we're still not giving up a whole day off, even if he needs a hand again later in the day."

The murmuring sounded speculative and positive. I heard snippets like "That could work."

I was about to make some promises, which I hoped Allan would agree with. Taking a deep breath, I went on, "Now, we're unskilled labor, so we're going to work cheap. If you help, you get fed. We'll have dinner here just to keep it simple. Is everyone good with that?"

"Mmmm!" and "Oh, yum!" sounded good with that; we'd all eaten Allan's cooking.

I'd found an old notebook and scribbled a quick grid on it. "I think we need two people a day, at least early on. I'm off Tuesday, so we need one more that day, and if we have three tomorrow and Monday, that might be even better. I don't know how much stuff he offloads from the food truck, but I know it gets there around eight a.m., and he has to be there."

"Where is 'there'?" Kurt asked.

"I don't know." I thought fast. "But he leaves here around seven forty-five and takes the shuttle, so not far. Meet him at the door at seven forty-five? And then dinner here at six thirty."

Someone grumbled about giving up sleep, but cut off mid-sentence, possibly because of my glare, possibly from someone's flying elbow. "If everyone helps a little, he can stay in business.

It's a good cause, right?" I wrote my name on a Tuesday slot and passed the notebook around. Kim wrote her name, then Julie, who handed the notebook over to Gabe. By the time I got it back, the woman had returned with the crutches and a week's worth of helping hands had been marked down. Some, like Chelsea, took two slots, and others, like Devon, only one, but we had it covered. If there was a day that turned out to be too lightly staffed, I'd twist some arms, or some of Allan's other friends might pitch in. Maybe I'd even take a day off and do it myself.

"Thanks, guys. He's conked out with a pain pill right now, or he'd tell you himself, but I know he'll be happy for the help. Thanks." People filed out, murmuring their dismay over what had happened. I looked over the list, grateful for my friends and their goodwill.

Jake and Kurt stopped for a moment on the way out the door. "Did, uh, that guy ever meet up with you?" Jake asked.

"Yeah. I need to get Monday off. I'm supposed to be in Phippsburg by one." Wanting to forget about the hearings, I hadn't devoted a lot of thought to it.

"How are you getting there?" Kurt had a motorbike, but road conditions were often bad enough that he used the shuttle or went with Jake in his beater Toyota.

"I'll figure something out." Maybe James Underwood could give me a lift. Yeah, right. More likely, I'd hit the Avis place out at the landing strip, drive some millionaire-worthy rental for half a day.

"You can use the Toyota if you need to," Jake offered. "It will get you there; it just looks awful."

His rusty brown Corolla looked bad enough he could have gotten a ticket for uglifying Wapiti Creek, but it was more wheels than I had. "Thanks. I may need to do that."

"Just find me for the keys."

Damn, I had some good friends. Jake just saved me a hundred bucks.

"Allan's a good guy, right?" Kurt could be asking because he wanted to know if he was spending his days off well, or because he was concerned for me getting involved with someone none of us knew.

"So far, yeah." That could cover both reasons. "I just hate that he got hurt. It was sort of because of an incident I could have handled better. I'm just glad everyone's willing to help him."

Jake shook his head. "Mark, think. We hardly know Allan. We're doing it for you."

It didn't matter why they were doing it; it was good with me as long as Allan got the help he needed.

No one else was around to hear Jake's last, quiet question. "Are you sleeping any better?"

"Yeah, I am." Memory supplied the interrupted bad dream. "Better when it's next to him." That got nods of understanding and then they were gone.

Allan was still asleep when I got back to his apartment and removed the cold packs, only turning over enough to throw an arm over my chest when I slipped back in beside him. Sleepily, or groggily, he returned the goodnight kiss and sighed back into his dreams.

Twice in the night I came to awareness. Around one in the morning Randi came home, quietly, but nothing could disguise the light that followed her through the open door. "Don't you guys have somewhere else to do that?" she grumbled softly when she spotted us, and then found her way to the bathroom and her bedroom in the dark.

Later, Allan roused, hurting, so I brought him another pill

and some water. The trip to the can was beyond him tonight, even with the crutches, so I assisted him there and back, then tucked him in again. His presence kept my sleep peaceful even after seeing him fall today, though I'd anticipated an ugly night. Taking care of Allan meant he was taking care of me, too. I kissed the back of his neck and slept a dreamless sleep.

FIFTEEN

Allan stretched without sitting up, and when he collapsed, even I felt the impact of the brace on his forehead. Hell, the downstairs neighbors probably felt it.

"Ouch. Crap, I forgot all about this." He held the arm over his head and glared before placing it cautiously on the pillow behind his head.

"Good. If you could forget it for a bit, it's not as bad as it could be." I ran my hand down his chest, then got up to bring more ice packs, which went against the injuries after I opened the Velcros for him. He'd need that a couple more times today before I saw him again, but one of the kitchen crew could help him. Better be Kim or Julie....

"Plenty bad. I have dinner for seventy-three to cook today, and half a body to do it with. I guess I'd better start calling cancellations." He met my eyes with a small smile, the sort that meant "I'm not going to howl out loud."

"Don't do that." I pulled him tight against me with the arm that wasn't propping me up.

"No choice. I might be able to scrape up some help for

tomorrow, but today…. Not possible, and I don't have the right product mix in the freezer to make it up." He shut his eyes, letting me brush my lips over his eyelids. "You're damned lovey in the face of disaster, Mark."

"If there was a disaster, I'd be doing something about it," I told him wickedly. "Kisses are for afterward." That hit me in the gut, given who I'd kissed after the last disaster, but Jake got shoved to the back of my mind really fast.

"Oh? Is it over, then?" He opened one eye. "And nobody mentioned it?"

"Everything but the healing. Your work crew today is—" I had to roll over to fish the paper out of my pocket. "Dave, Kim, and Laura. Tomorrow, Kurt, Julie, and Gabe." Speaking of which, they'll be waiting for you at the door for the 7:50 shuttle, because we aren't sure where the kitchen is." None of the cinnamon roll friends had known either.

He snatched the paper out of my hand. "What? Who?" Studying the sheet answered some of the questions, maybe raised more. "How?"

"You were out like a light, so I rounded everyone up and explained. We've got you covered for a week, and we'll do it again if you need it." Ignoring that small voice that suggested this was a big promise for other people to fulfill, I reassured him that his business wouldn't founder. "Will work for food, you know?"

"For food…. You mean, I just feed them. I mean, you?" He goggled at me. "Or what?"

"Yeah. Just feed the crew. We have to work cheap because some of us probably need coaching on which end of the knife to hold. But we can pour, stir, and lift the pots." My own skills were on the rudimentary side, but even I could manage that much. "Just tell us where, what, and when."

"You think? Mark, a sixty-five quart stockpot weighs as much as an adult when it's full."

"Then make Dave and Kim lift it. It will be worth it for good soup." I sat up and pulled him upright, too. "You are making soup today, aren't you?"

"Yeah…." he agreed uncertainly. "I'll just hop around giving directions…." Then he spotted the crutches, leaning against the wall within touching distance. "You thought of everything." He reached out to prod the unpadded handle, then turned back to me. "Thanks, Mark. This would be a lot harder without all you've done."

"It's what lovers do, isn't it? Take care of each other?" I rubbed his bristly cheek with one hand.

"It is, but…. We just started seeing each other, so it's just… a lot for so early." He leaned into my hand. Maybe it was, but —I could do something for Allan, so I would. There were others I couldn't help, but I pushed that thought aside.

"It isn't as if we could pencil you in a disaster for April. This way you know how I behave." I leaned down for a smooch. "Then you can throw me out early if you can't stand it."

He laughed. "How hard did you twist that woman's tail to get the ER bill paid?"

"Just suggested that you might sue if things went bad. Of course, she may have seen the blood in my eye." I pulled him back against me, wishing there was more time before the shuttle. "We need to get you up and dressed, damn it. Me too. I have to patrol today, or I'd be on your kitchen crew. How's the pain?"

"Hmm, I think ibuprofen ought to do it, at least for starters. There's some in the bathroom cabinet."

Before returning with a handful of tablets and a glass of

water, I left a dab of toothpaste on his toothbrush. He might not be able to manage the twisty top.

"Need a hand cleaning up?" I waggled my eyebrows while adjusting the height of the crutches for him.

"I'd like that, but we'll be late, if one thing leads to another. I can manage. Hold the thought for later, okay?" He swung out an experimental step on the crutches, then headed into the bathroom. "Honest, Mark, I can take care of things in here!" Allan laughed, but there was an undertone of irritation when he first pulled me close for a kiss and then shoved me out and shut the door. Really, I was just trying to help.

Okay, trusting that he can manage for the few minutes it would take for me to buzz through my place and get dressed. I was back in time to get us fed and down to the door, where Kim, Dave, and one of the cinnamon roll friends waited.

"We'll take good care of him," Kim assured me with a wink I pretended not to see. I helped him up the steps into the van.

"Relax," Dave advised me quietly. "Allan's a big boy."

Relaxed was not me as the shuttle drove away to the east. In the flurry of getting ready, I'd forgotten to get Allan's number or the address of the kitchen. If I needed to, I could just call Kim and take the teasing. The sick feeling in my gut suggested I'd need to.

SIXTEEN

My supervisor needed to know about my legal issues. I'd need some time off to give testimony. Subpoena in an inside pocket, I ran back down to catch the westbound shuttle to the patrol hut, my skis, and too damned much that kept me away from Allan. Marty held the door open to let me skid into the van.

"Hey, Marty, how are you getting to Phippsburg?" Borrowing Jake's car might not be the only option, and Marty had to be there, too. The fancy SUVs and elegant sedans on the street around us mocked me with my lack of transportation.

"I called the resort van service. It won't cost more than a day's pay," he replied glumly. "Unless you have a better idea?"

"You can ride with me. Jake offered the Toyota."

"Hey, better being seen in the crapmobile than spending the money." We laughed together for the first time in days. "Guess we need to leave by noon?"

"That should be enough time. Wonder if Ben wants us to patrol tomorrow morning?" As long as I didn't try to bring up specifics, Marty and I were probably okay again. He'd avoided me yesterday, convincing me he was serious about not discussing the grand jury. I could wait. He'd be a captive audience tomorrow in the car.

At the patrol hut we hailed our boss. "When do you need to be there?" Ben asked, looking at the paperwork. "Okay, no problem. Go hit the slopes, Marty. Mark, I need you in the office." Heart sinking, I followed him in.

"Shut the door and sit down, Mark. This isn't the only problem you have." Ben pulled out a different paper. "What exactly did you say to Mrs. Underwood?"

"I told her that I wasn't going to tell the grand jury any lies to make it all come out the way she wanted." My stomach hit the floor. "Why?"

"Was that everything? Because she's filed a complaint against you, citing unprofessional conduct. Inappropriate remarks about her sex life. And yours." Ben's eyes were hard. "Which doesn't sound like you, but she was pretty riled. What exactly did you say to her?"

"She caught me the day before yesterday on the lift and accused me of killing Ulf on her husband's orders. Like an avalanche is a good weapon, and like I'd do it at all." This couldn't possibly be covered by the grand jury; this happened after. I told myself that firmly and explained further. "Then yesterday she grabbed me again and started out hinting that she was behind this stuff." I tapped the subpoenas. "She kept asking if I'd gotten anything unusual, and I finally got mad enough to say I'd gotten laid." I was ashamed of invoking Allan like that then, and more so now, but I hadn't mentioned names or details.

"Is the term 'fuck-buddy' one you usually use to members of the public?"

"No." I couldn't truthfully deny that I had used it once.

"Just to the boss's wife?" Ben sounded scandalized at the choice.

"The boss's soon-to-be ex-wife, but yeah, her."

"Mark. You are smarter than that, and you've gone stupid on me. You're the guy who's supposed to be calm and reasonable on the slopes, yet you obviously got into it big time with someone who knows the expectations around here. It doesn't matter about her future; the only thing I can go off is what happened. And apparently it happened pretty much the way she said." Ben tossed the sheet of paper at me. "I don't have a lot of choice, except between suspending you and firing you."

"Firing me?" I jerked upright to stare at him.

"I don't want to do that. You sound like you were provoked on some pretty deep levels. But yes, those are the rules, which we both knew when you hired on. So…." Ben stopped for a deep breath. "One week suspension, no pay. And when you come back, watch your mouth, and for heaven's sake stay away from her."

"I've been trying to stay away from her." The cold started in my gut and spread up and down through me. "She's been after me."

"Doesn't matter; you still can't mouth off like that." He handed me a paper. "Sign it and go tell Devon where he's supposed to be, and any special stuff he needs to know. He's covering for you this week."

I was so stunned by this fresh mess that Devon had to prompt me three times to spit out the correct radio frequencies. He listened carefully to my warnings about liquored-up movie stars and other hazards. Then I turned to go, half wondering if I'd left something important out and not able to care enough to think what it could be.

"Hey, Mark?" Devon called me back. "You know I didn't

want to get a place on the patrol like this…."

"I know, but you're qualified, and if someone has to, better you than some others I could name." One of them was out now, covering for an injured patroller. Might as well ask now—it would give the hamsters in my mind fresh wheels to run on, wheels that didn't squeak *Why didn't you keep your big mouth shut?* "Why didn't you take the spot at Monarch?"

"Better snow, better slopes here. And there's a girl at Monarch who…." He stopped, making me remember that he almost never talked about himself. "Need an engagement ring, never worn?"

"No, not this week." I marked one more trouble spot on his map—I had forgotten to mention something. "See you later."

"Yeah. Any idea what Allan's making?" He brightened.

"Don't know. But it will be good." Suddenly I wondered if the whole kitchen squad expected to be fed every day. I might have been unclear. What if that's how they'd taken it? Better warn Allan. In person. That was the one improvement in my day; I could chop vegetables or something.

The shuttle took me and my mixed bag of thoughts back to the apartment, where I shed the outdoor gear and put on some jeans. At least the polyprope hadn't marinated on me yet. Now to track down my guy. I picked up the phone and dialed the one number I knew had Allan near the other end. "Hey, Kim!" She'd answered after the fourth ring. "Where are you?"

"Elbow deep in celery, where'd you think?" she shot back.

"Where are you and the celery? I'll come join you."

"Third and Cottontail, the old Haricots Verts building. Come in through the back. Hey, aren't you wor—"

"See you in a bit!" I cut the call off in spite of more questions.

Judging from the luscious scent of browning beef, Allan was

busy polluting the defunct vegetarian restaurant. The back door was open; I entered to happy greetings. "Yay, more help!"

"Hi, guys!" The rest of my greetings were non-verbal, once I got my hands on my man. I needed to touch someone who liked me, and maybe I overdid it, but Allan wasn't objecting. Not even. Big hugs and a big kiss later, we established that Allan and I had missed each other, and that Kim and Dave were spoilsports.

"I'd give that an eight-point-five, Kim," Dave intoned in his best announcer's voice. He held a ladle like a microphone, first to his face and then to Kim's.

Kim disagreed. "That should get a two-tenths bonus for style, Dave." For that, I flipped them off and kissed Allan again.

"Oh noes, Kim, interaction with spectators is a big five-tenths deduct, so the final score is eight-point-two!" Dave dropped the ladle on the work table; the metallic ringing mixed with their laughter. Laura laughed and shook her head at the lot of us.

"I can't do better than eight-point-five with my clothes on anyway," Allan whispered. That doubled me over on his shoulder, laughing.

Once I got my voice back, I just told them, "Put me to work, guys." Softly into Allan's ear, I added, "You'll show me later."

"You bet." He let me go and pointed to a pile of potatoes Laura was working on. "In the meantime, peel and dice small."

While we dealt with the potatoes, Allan crutched from person to person, offering directions, demonstrating knife work, and supervising us mixing this with that, creating tantalizing aromas in huge amounts. Seventy-three dinners, he'd said, more with the kitchen volunteers' meals. I did mention that we might have a lot more people than the current crew.

"No problem. There's stuff in the freezer."

"Okay, spill it. Why are you here and not halfway down Sundance?" Kim asked, once we put tin pans of macaroni and cheese into the ovens. Preparation wasn't anything like the blue box sort, for sure.

"I've been suspended for a whole week," I reported glumly. "Due to that lovely conversation I had with Melanie Underwood. She ratted me out after she pushed me hard." Everybody turned to stare at me with little gasps. "But hey!" I wanted to divert the conversation to the brighter side. "I can be useful here when I'm not in Phippsburg."

I came to stand near Allan, who was perched on a barstool. I'd stolen it from the dark, barely heated dining area, where tables and chairs waited forlornly for diners who weren't coming. Glassware remained in racks, though no liquor bottles stood before the mirror, and a television looked down with a blank face at a couch. The barstool might have gone unoccupied for months before I took it to the kitchen, the only bright part of the building.

"And you have to be there when?" Allan slipped his arm around my waist.

"Marty and I have to be at the courthouse by one tomorrow." With my arm over his shoulder, I felt strong enough to cope with the prospect. "I can be an amateur chef in the morning again."

"I'll take you in the van, since we'll be all done except for oven time." Allan patted his pocket, where keys jingled softly. "Though you'll have to drive."

"You don't have to stir the soup or anything?" Not that I'd say it out loud, but I really wanted a hand to hold and Allan's hand most of all.

"It isn't substantially different from grabbing a few runs,

and someone who isn't directly involved should know what's going on." Laura, Kim, and Dave all muttered agreement. "Any idea how long you guys will be?"

"Last time it was only about fifteen minutes each." Last time, no one had been gunning for us. "That was the coroner's hearing, though. This could be longer."

He patted my hip. "If it drags on long enough to be a problem, I'll get the deliveries done, then come back for you."

If we weren't in jail, that would work fine. Would they do that before the grand jury finished? Would they think we were material witnesses? Flight risks? Every *CSI* episode I'd ever watched rattled in my head.

"That's great." I kissed the side of his head, to a chorus of "awww" from the others. They didn't give Marty and Chelsea this much grief when they were new and all lovey. Oh, yeah, we did.

"And now you guys get to learn about dish pit." Allan brought us back to the task at hand. "I get all the pots and utensils clean before I head out to ski, or used to." He gave the wrist brace a sour look. "Otherwise it gets crusty and takes three times as much work, besides the sanitation issues. Here's what you do...."

With my arms in soapy water to the elbow, I considered that Allan might find help with cleanup the best part of all.

Once the last rack of pots slid into the sanitizer, we considered what to do next. "Do you need us back later to load and deliver?" Laura asked. "What time should we be here?"

"I'll be here anyway." Allan would need me this afternoon, I knew, and I didn't have to be anywhere else, thanks to Melanie, that bitch.

"Penny comes in at four, so I think the three of us are good. I really appreciate the help today, and tonight you get to taste the fruits of your labors." Allan had calculated the extra food for the helpers to be distributed into the tins for the oven.

"Yeah, my place about six thirty." Naughty ideas were percolating in my head—I wanted this gang out of here now. "See you later!"

They left, Dave and Kim making bets about the afternoon's football game. Allan and I were alone in the hot kitchen. It was almost too hot to hug him, which I mentioned with my lips to his ear.

"Let's go to the bar," Allan suggested. "It's nippy, but there's still a couch in there."

It was chilly enough that the dustcover over the couch might get used for a blanket, but it was a lot more comfortable than the barstool in the hot kitchen. I carried our plates, and we ate sandwiches Allan had thrown together one handed over my protestation of help. He didn't object to me pulling him across my lap, though, and kissed me back with enough heat to rival any furnace.

"This just might be doable, Mark," he sighed in a lull. "With the helpers you gathered, I think I can keep going until I'm healed up."

"Quit thinking about business. You aren't exactly alone now." His erection grew inside his clothing as I played with him from outside the fabric, shifting and rolling him through the layers. We had all afternoon—we could take it slow.

"Damned good thing." His voice had gone hoarse.

Just… damned good. My hand found the gap between waistband and warm skin and slipped inside to still be separated from him by boxers, though they gapped to let me touch skin through the fly. He was so hard under my hand, yet smooth and soft. His balls rolled under my fingers with every little movement, his cock pressed to my palm. Allan's tongue met mine swipe for swipe. Our mouths roamed against each other's faces, and his good hand twined into my hair. I pulled him farther into my lap and had to retreat far enough to undo his fly just for enough room, but our mouths stayed together.

There were more things to do to him. Now I worked his cock and balls out of his clothing, the better to wrap my long fingers around him and pump him slowly. The room was cold enough I wouldn't undress him more. His responses showed me what he liked. A thumb rubbing over the slit, opening it and spreading the droplets of precome over the head, got a gasp and a small cry into my mouth, while fingers on either side of the base of his shaft brought moans more like contentment. I swallowed all his sounds and found ways to get more out of him.

Suddenly the sound he gave me was a shout of, "Not yet! Not yet!" He wrenched his mouth away. Stilling my hand, I let him back away from his climax with my lips now pressed to his forehead. "I want…," he started, but I'd stolen too much of his breath for him to tell me yet, so while he gulped in the air, I slid my hand farther into his clothing, traveling past his balls and tickling over the flat place to his crack. He spread his thighs to let me explore, touching the small ridges of his pucker and the soft skin near it. Small swirls and tiny presses, but not pressing in, made him buck and then push back against me.

"What do you want?" I murmured into his hair, never stopping the little strokes and promises against his hole.

"That's making me want something bigger in there," he murmured back, spreading his legs wider. "But we aren't prepared. I never thought of needing stuff here."

He opened enough to let my fingertip in, which made me gulp for air myself. "Tonight, then. Want me to suck you?"

"Always, Mark. Ohhhh…." I wiggled my finger a tiny bit, wary of dryness, and slipped out again, wishing he was slick and

I could plunge in deeply instead. This couch was going to get all sorts of things stuffed into the cushions, just so I wouldn't have to get up and search for anything here, ever. There would be more private afternoons this week, provided I wasn't in jail.

Allan lay flat against the cushions when I slid out from under him to kneel on the floor. Brushing my lips over his forehead and then taking his mouth again while leaning against his broad chest let me luxuriate in his strong embrace. It took a long time to wiggle free and nibble my way down his chest, and only the thought of his cock getting chilly in the unheated air made me try to get loose.

"Has it turned into a popsicle yet?" I warmed him with breath and lips. "Let me show you what I do with popsicles."

I was going to do all the work, to rouse him and bring him to orgasm, but there was no keeping his hips still. Even with hands on his thigh and belly he writhed and thrust to meet my mouth. I gave up and let him help me make him crazy.

"Come up here; let me suck you, too." Allan fumbled at my fly one handed, and together we got my jeans down far enough that he could, once I climbed up and straddled his head. Oh man, damn. Even if I had to arch my back rather high to avoid either of us getting bent backwards too far.

He caught my cock in his mouth. Doing to me what I was doing to him shut my mind down to everything but how good it all felt. I had one arm wrapped around his thigh, reminding me that I'd been farther inside his clothing. Back under his jeans I went, finding his hole to tease more, making him break the rhythm on me. Squeezing my ass hard with his good hand, he pulled me away enough that he lost my cock again.

"I can't concentrate when you do that." He buried his face into my thigh and let me do what I wanted.

Must have been what he wanted, too, because soon he

rippled in my mouth, filling it with his come, screaming against my leg. I waited him out, loving his loss of control, until he finally relaxed against the cushions, and I flipped around to kiss him.

"Good?" I knew he could taste traces of himself on my lips.

"Wonderful. Let me demonstrate." He tried to wiggle out from under me, but I'd do the work. Once again I was straddling his head, but I could look down into his face now as I hung on to the arm of the couch. One foot on the floor and I could move any way he wanted me. Allan wanted me slow and playful, then he wanted me fast and steady, thrusting into his hand and his mouth. His free hand left my hip to find my crack from outside my jeans. He pressed fingertips up; he'd be inside me if not for the clothing, and I'd have welcomed him in. It made me thrust harder, to meet him on the backstroke, too, and suddenly I was exploding, coming, collapsing.

"Good?" He knew the answer just as I had, though I nodded while trying to get a breath deep enough to speak. He held me, rubbing my back while I recovered, and I would have lain against him for the rest of the afternoon if my exposed cheeks hadn't been frosting over. Reluctantly, I got up and fixed my clothing, then tried to do his, but he was already there.

"I can do it, Mark." Allan caught my hand and nibbled the knuckles. "Let's go wash our hands, stir the soup, and decide which game to watch, or do you want to do other stuff? That TV works."

"It's the playoffs." Which didn't matter much to me—what I really wanted was to be very, very close to the one part of my life that wasn't screwed up beyond belief. Penny found us huddled up together on the couch under the dustcover, yelling about the tied score.

SEVENTEEN

"Don't bleed on the yams!" Allan swung my hand away from the vegetables, slapping a towel over the wound in nearly the same motion. I'd been chopping vigorously, imagining Melanie, author of my misery, under the blade. If I'd had enough sleep my aim would have been better.

"Gabe, get the yams. Mark can have the carrot scraper." He helped me clean and bandage the cut, and sent me back to a tool that I couldn't hurt myself with. "You're getting chef's hands."

Scrapes, cuts, a couple of encounters with hot pots… yeah, I was catching up with him. My concentration wasn't the best it had ever been, and several cups of coffee were helping only marginally. I'd watched Allan sleep most of the night, after I put him to bed with a pain pill, worn out and hurting from the full day of cooking, deliveries, and then serving dinner to the gang. He'd swatted me away when I tried to dish out the food and then paid for overdoing it. I wouldn't let him do that again.

"Sit down, Mark." Julie took over the scolding, just because I tried to get the spices down from the shelf for him. "You're hovering." I sat back with the scraper, and when Allan started hunting in the drawer, Julie kicked my ankle before I got all the way up to dig whatever it was he wanted out for him. I didn't recognize the thing he produced, but he could have explained what it looked like. Kurt was at the stove, stirring the sauce, but he gave me the warning eyebrow too. Some friends, getting in the way of me taking care of Allan.

They wouldn't even let me answer the phone, though Gabe might have had a point about me not knowing what to say after "Almost Home Catering. Dinner will be good tonight." Stripping the skins off carrots was a poor substitute, and when an orange sliver flew a little too far and stuck to Julie's arm, I was ticked enough not to say anything. Everyone looked at me funny and got real quiet when I started chopping the vegetables into bite-sized chunks.

The phone was ringing a lot, too, and Allan had to say three different times, "Yes, the website isn't working, sorry." That sounded like a real problem, one I didn't know how to fix. After the last of those calls, he muttered, "Damned website. More trouble than it's worth."

"I could take a look." Gabe had finished chopping yams and stirred them into a bigger pot with other things. He glanced over to the computer where Allan had entered some orders and printed off some slips.

"That would be great. It's more hindrance than help right now, and it's supposed to save me all sorts of time, which it isn't." Allan clicked a couple times with the mouse. "What do you need?"

"The password to get into the guts of the site, and it would help to know what it's built with." Gabe came to look.

"It was supposed to be some easy-to-use template thing. Password is L-e-N-C-e-V-2." Allan looked worried. Gabe sat down and started opening windows. Biting my lip hard, I said nothing as someone else did what Allan needed most, trying to tell myself I was the one who'd introduced him to help.

"It might be saved in your FTP software. Oh good, the address is in there." Clicking, tapping, and mumbling followed. "The password is all caps?"

"The Es are lower case." Allan looked worried, as if maybe that wasn't the right answer.

"Aha! We're in! What do you want it to do?" Gabe started clicking through screens and grimacing.

"Best case, display the day's menus, allow for selection, number of people to feed, address, and payment. It would be heaven if it would print out delivery tickets from that." Allan sounded wistful. He returned to the prep area to adjust the heat once we put pans into the oven.

"That seems pretty basic. Let me play with it this afternoon, okay?" Gabe looked up for a scant second before his fingers flew over the keys again.

"Sure. Stir the soup a couple of times if you're going to be here anyway." Allan crutched back over to me. "Drop those carrots in the sauce, stir to coat, and then they go in the low temp oven, Mark." He ran his fingers over the back of my neck, which the hairnet left strangely exposed. "Do you need to run by the apartment to change clothes?"

"I should. I'm spattered and this isn't appropriate for court." I gave him a wry look on my way to the oven with the carrot pans. "Marty will meet us there."

"Okay, I'll meet you at the van. Thanks, guys. Do I have a volunteer for delivery?" He looked at everybody but me. I cleared my throat. "Just in case things run long?"

Great. My lover thought I might be in jail before the day

was out. He could get his own damned spices down off the shelf.

"I will." Allan nodded acknowledgement to Kurt and crutched off toward the restroom. Once he was sort of out of earshot, Kurt turned to me. "Don't baby him, Mark. He's injured, not broken, brain-damaged, or incompetent."

"I'm just taking care of him while he's hurt!" I wasn't sticking around to hear anything else about relationships from Mr. Super-competent, who skied, chopped meat, and managed his lover's sexual experiences all to some sort of Olympic standard. I slammed out the back door and got most of the way to the van before I realized I'd left my parka—the blue one, not the patrol burgundy one I'd had to leave behind at the staff hut yesterday morning. Conversation halted abruptly when I came back in just long enough to grab the jacket, which I didn't put on until a door separated me from the busybodies inside.

Allan's gentle hand on my arm made me yank my forehead away from the van window where I'd been leaning, trying not to think of the shambles my life might be in a few hours. "Are you okay to drive?"

"Yeah. Of course," I said, but it wasn't true until I'd held him for a few minutes and stolen a kiss that wasn't all about passion.

Marty sat gingerly on the upturned crate that served for a third seat in the van. "Just don't take any sudden corners, okay?"

He'd had the same idea I had about dressing: dark slacks and a turtleneck, though he'd thrown a nice sweater over it and I had a camel hair jacket. Allan had changed, too, though he wasn't appearing in court. It was the first time I'd seen him in slacks and a jacket. It looked good on him.

"I won't." It had been a month or two since I'd driven anything, so caution was in order.

"Old Betsy here probably couldn't take it." Allan patted the dashboard. "Once I have another good month, she gets some new shock absorbers."

The ride to Phippsburg was quiet, with a little small talk between Allan and Marty. I concentrated on the winding road, knowing there was nothing Marty would discuss about our coming testimony, and nothing I wanted to say to Allan with Marty around to hear it.

The courthouse parking lot had a few slots open. I let Allan off at the door before parking. He waited for me and Marty to park, which was my big opportunity for collusion. "The truth, the whole truth, nothing but the truth," I told Marty. "Just like last time." The van was too far to the right in the parking spot, so I pulled back out and tried again; otherwise, Marty wouldn't be able to get out.

"Right." He looked at me strangely, like he'd been expecting something different.

"I like the truth just fine. I also like not being accused of murder or accessory to murder, or collusion about murder, or whatever the hell it's called." My last words were suddenly loud when I cut the engine.

"That's convenient, since we didn't do anything wrong." Marty was trying to get the door to slide open.

"Like that is going to protect us with Melanie Underwood and her tame DA on our case." I discovered yesterday that the door wouldn't open from the inside; Marty would have to wait until I opened it for him.

"You really think that?" Marty turned to look at me, his glasses catching the light.

"You have another explanation for why she came after us on the lifts like that, the timing, and the way she got me suspended? She wants a chunk of her husband on a plate and thinks we're going to give it to her."

"My dad thinks Simon Calhoun is pretty honest." He rattled the door handle again. "Go around and open this, okay?"

"If your dad can monitor all the petty politics around here from two states away, he's damned good. Maybe Calhoun is honest, but you don't think Melanie could sell him an idea?" I didn't move.

"But can she sell it to the grand jurors? That's the point of the grand jury, to keep it from being the sole call of the DA." Marty leaned back on his heels. "Come on, open the door."

"I'd have slept better last night if you'd mentioned that, pal." My seatbelt retracted with a clank.

"Sorry. I thought you knew."

"Grand juries and stuff like that might have been your dinner talk growing up, but not mine." I finally let him out. The door slid over with a brain-twisting squeak. "I just want the truth to keep us free."

"Have some faith, Mark." Marty walked beside me to the door where Allan waited for us. Marty checked his paperwork and directed us to the second floor, where a bailiff waited.

"Mark McAvoy, Martin Tanquist." He ticked us off his list and turned to Allan. "Are you counsel? You two do know he can't go in?"

"No, just a friend," Allan told him.

"You can wait with them, but no talking." He led us to a

small room with a table and some chairs. "The judge will be along in a few minutes. Have a seat."

Allan let me lean his crutches against the wall. Glad for his presence, I pulled my chair very close to him, and I imagined Marty wished Chelsea could have been there, too. Holding hands seemed like a really good idea just then, because the pressure on my fingers might distract me from the cramping in my gut, not that this was a good venue for public displays of affection. I slid my foot over until my shoe was tight against Allan's brace. He smiled reassuringly at me and slipped his hand under the table until our fingers linked. The clock on the wall ticked away ten more minutes before anything else happened.

Allan sat without fidgeting, only giving a little squeeze with his fingers now and then. Grateful for the contact, I took a deep breath and tried to empty my mind of everything. Fogged with lack of sleep last night, it was hard to stop the whirl of thoughts. I'd been terrified of what I'd dream, fearful of extra vividness, as if I needed to see that scene any more clearly. Had I been confident Allan would rouse and wake me, I would have risked more than the intermittent dozing when fatigue got the better of me, but with that pain pill on board, he might not have come alert. I lay against him, counting time by the rise and fall of his chest.

The bailiff reappeared. "Mr. McAvoy? Come with me." With a last pinkie squeeze from Allan, I rose for what I was afraid would be my last walk as anything but a murder suspect. Once in the small, plain courtroom, the bailiff clicked the little gate on the witness box shut behind me with a prophetic *snick*.

EIGHTEEN

Everyone who wasn't in a box, that is, everyone but me and the dozen people sitting in the much bigger box to one side, was milling around, chatting, rustling papers, and acting like this was just some pleasant day at the office. After a few minutes, they sorted themselves out into a few people I didn't recognize and only one I did, and that from pictures. Simon Calhoun pulled the knot of his tie down another inch, the only informal note between him, the sharply creased court reporter, the robed judge, and two people who were there for who-the-hell-knew-why. I didn't have anyone there who was on my side, for sure. The one thing I knew about grand juries was that I couldn't bring a lawyer in with me, not that I had one. Not that I could afford one.

Please, Lord, let me not need them to appoint one at the county's expense.

Simon Calhoun cleared his throat and suggested, "Shall we get on with this?" Everyone drew to attention, more or less, and he went on. "Mr. McAvoy, a grand jury tends to be a lot more relaxed affair than anything you've seen on the television, so we'll ask you some questions and you'll tell us the answers, no big deal." Right. "Do you—" One of the unidentified men jumped up and stuck a leather-bound Bible out at me, where I dutifully, if skeptically, placed my hand. "Do you swear to tell the truth, the whole truth, and nothing but the truth?"

"I do." That was with or without the Bible.

"Please state your whole name for the record. Spell the last name."

"Mark Thomas McAvoy, M-C...."

The DA asked questions I expected: some basics of who I was, what did I do, and why was I qualified to do it.

"So, Mr. McAvoy, are all the ski patrols at Wapiti Creek qualified to work the snow conditions team as well?"

I thought of one or two who barely qualified to notice anything outside their own beautiful selves, let alone a mountain ready to trigger. "No, I don't think so."

"What makes you qualified, then?"

"Experience that dates back to what amounted to an apprenticeship with Karl Wolters starting when I was fourteen. Dr. Wolters is now head of the Utah Avalanche Center." I had to add that when no one looked suitably impressed. "I've recertified with the Utah Avalanche Center four times on backcountry conditions, and I have a degree in snow sciences from the University of Montana."

Someone laughed. It wasn't the first time I'd gotten that reaction.

"Tell us about that, please." Simon Calhoun was not the one laughing, though he did seem amused.

"It's a specialty through the earth science department, and the bachelor's requires calculus, physics, chemistry, statistics, geography, cartography, geology, and a couple of engineering classes. I didn't ski my way through it." Whoa, got to keep a lid on the defensiveness.

"I imagine not," Calhoun said, and he'd quit smiling. "So, all that science and enough skiing expertise to patrol on a demanding mountain." Some of the people in the jury box were paying sharp attention.

"Yes." I could see this leading up to *If you're so good, how'd you end up with a dead body?*

"Tell us about why you'd set an avalanche on a ski slope." He hitched a hip on the lawyers' table, which didn't relax me any.

"We'd do it if there was a danger of an unplanned slide. Slopes with cornices above are notorious for that. A cornice is an unsupported shelf of snow built by the wind; if it falls, it can knock several layers loose. The snowpack has layers of different strengths and adhesion—they may not stick to each other—and that creates instability. That might not become a problem until more snow has deposited on top. The strength of the layers can change with time, depending on what falls on top, the wind conditions, and the sun exposure. That sort of terrain tends to be really attractive to the skiers, so you try to minimize the danger." I wondered what to do with my hands and finally rested them flat on my thighs.

"How do you assess the strength of a snow layer?" Calhoun looked nothing but interested.

"The quick and dirty way is by checking hardness—it's an official scale. You stick your fingers into the snow horizontally. A hard layer might let you only put one or two fingers in; with a really soft layer you can push your whole fist in." Maybe the court reporter couldn't catch my demonstration, but the jury did. "The layer may change with time, compression, and temperature." I'd dug a lot of pits in the backcountry to look at six vertical feet of snow, keeping careful records of what was happening at the bottom of the snowpack.

"How does this apply to the run called Cement Chute?" Calhoun got to the meat of the matter, and there was a lot of movement in the jury box. I glanced at them, reminding myself that they lived in the Colorado mountains—they had to have some basic notion of how snow behaved.

"A large cornice forms regularly over the top, which we try to keep sawed down, because the snowboarders want to use it for a ramp. Even if it fell and didn't take the slope with it, just the cornice coming down could hurt someone. That happened at Alta not too long ago." The memory gave me the shivers; I'd heard about it from a friend who'd had to dig. "We have to balance that against the other conditions, because bouncing the cornice off the slope provides the most specific trigger. Otherwise, we might be getting slides on more hillsides than we want."

Calhoun checked some notes. "Because...?"

"The noise from the howitzer isn't directional. When we fire that, we risk taking down slopes where no one has been kept away by anything better than their own good sense, though we do announce our intentions ahead of time. But we can't be sure everyone has gotten the news, even though we post the off-piste danger zones. We do know where they are for each of the slopes we have to shoot."

"When do you normally set avalanches?" Guess someone in the jury was impatient. Calhoun didn't shush him, which surprised me.

"We do it when we have an unstable slope." Didn't I just say that?

"I mean, what time of day?" The fiftysomething man in the ski sweater persisted.

Right into the problem. "We try to do it early, before the lifts open to the skiers."

"Think back to a slide on Cement Chute back in November, Mr. McAvoy." Like I could think of anything else. Thanks, Mr. Calhoun. "Was there more than one on that slope in that month?"

"Just one."

"What time of day was that?" He looked politely interested in the answer.

"About eleven a.m., and yes, the lifts were open."

"Please explain why you chose that time to do it."

I felt the abyss open below my feet. "We, Martin Tanquist and I, didn't choose it so much as it just happened that way. There had been several storms in the preceding few days, with about thirty-three inches of new snow, all on top of a layer of hoar—"

A couple people in the jury box snickered. Okay, it was usually funny to me, too.

"Leaving the technical discussion aside, that's a layer that other snow doesn't stick to very well. One of the storms was really wet, and then that layer was insulated by another layer of powder, so it didn't chill enough to freeze to the hoar well, because of the way the slope faces. So, we had that slope closed off, because we wanted to get enough weight on the slab to take that layer of hoar off too when it slid, so we'd get a better snow pack there after the next storm. That's why we didn't trigger it the few days prior.

"The day we went to trigger, several things happened that delayed us, and we'd have waited until the next morning, except that the lift operators were reporting that they were afraid the holiday skiers would use that slope anyway. Killy's Knees, which is a blue/black slope next to it, is the only safe way down for the folks who can't do expert runs, and we couldn't close that or guarantee that no one would just waltz past the barriers. We were really concerned that with the doubled crowd, someone would get by and get hurt."

"Tell us about the delays, Mr. McAvoy."

I sighed. "We got up to the top early, about an hour before lift opening, which should have been plenty of time. You have to understand, we were in full backcountry kit, with avalanche vests, snorkels, probes, beacons, shovels, all in all, about twenty-five pounds of gear, and it's bulky."

"Snorkels?" asked a woman in the jury. "Like scuba?"

"No, it's a tube that you strap across your body; it vents out behind you and well below your face. One way to die in an avalanche is to suffocate in your own exhalations. There's enough air, usually, but the carbon dioxide builds up around you and kills you if you're there long enough. So, you breathe in from the air around you and exhale so it goes behind you. It's saved lives. There's a brand name but we call them snorkels." I'd felt vindicated about insisting on the extra equipment after two men with snorkels had been buried in a slide up by Vail last year and were recovered alive after four hours. It wasn't luck, it was preparedness.

"Go on, please." Simon Calhoun interrupted my paean to planning.

"We got to the top of the West Peak, skied to the cornice, and started to saw. What should have happened is that the cornice came down, started the slab moving. Oh, the slab is the layers of snow that will come down, and it starts as a unit before it breaks apart." I responded to the question I thought one man was snaking his hand up to ask.

"But what did happen is that one of the snow saws, which are long, flexible blades with handles, broke after one good yank. Usually no big issue; we each had one. So Marty got his saw out and we kept going. That would have worked, except that we managed to drop the second one over the cornice, out of reach; it was just too dangerous to try to get it back. So, we had to go back and get another one. Or two.

"Going back was a lot harder than getting there, because it was a long uphill trudge back to Killy's Knees, and then down to the bottom of the mountain, which is about a half hour run in full kit, which means sort of cross-country skis, not downhill skis. Good for the trudge, not so good for the slope at speed. By the time we got to the bottom, the lifts were open. The snow-cats should have had a half hour already to groom Cement Chute by then, and you can bet they were annoyed at waiting around for us to call them." Pant, pant. Damn, I'd just dropped a lot of information on them.

"So you went straight back up with a new saw?"

I shook my head, realized that the court reporter couldn't catch that, and spoke. "No, it wasn't that simple. We didn't get back until later."

"Explain, please." Calhoun's questions didn't give me a minute.

"You're aware that patrollers are kind of cops on the slope?" Some of the jury nodded, one grimaced, and I wondered what his beef was, and with whom. Maybe even me? "But around here, we can't discipline the skiers as much as some resorts, or the celebrities get miffed and don't come back with all their nice money that makes jobs for us all. So things that would get tickets pulled elsewhere just get a brief sentence to a patroller's workshop on ski etiquette, and then they go back to terrorizing everyone else. It has to be pretty bad before we actually pull a ticket, like 'someone gets hurt' bad." I'd have been really angry if I'd had to let the woman who ran Allan down just get away with a warning. I thought of him, waiting back with Marty, and felt a rush of courage.

"The ones who misbehave just badly enough get to sit one of our classes before they can get back out. We also have 'know before you go' classes, for the ones smart enough to be prepared to go off-piste. Marty had one of those scheduled, and I had to lecture the idiots."

The laughter in the jury box told me I'd really said that out loud. I smiled at them, hoping to build some rapport. The only thing I did know about the grand jurors was that they had to be residents in the county, which meant they weren't likely to be rampaging rich people who probably got out of such civic duties without a qualm.

"Who were your idiots that day?" asked a lady juror, but she got shushed.

"Let's stick to the topic and refrain from name-calling." Calhoun looked sternly at the jury, then at me. "You, too, Mr. McAvoy. Go on about the events of the morning."

Abashed, I went on. "We had to get out of our equipment and lock it up, teach our classes, get kitted up again, and go back to the top of the mountain. We wanted to leave it for the next morning, but Gabe Wilson and the other lift attendants were radioing down that there were people coming off the lifts who had to be warned away from Cement Chute and might try it anyway. We didn't think it was safe to leave it, so back we went."

"And as it turned out, it wasn't safe to trigger, either. Tell us about that." The typing from the court reporter's odd little machine was suddenly loud.

"We stationed another patroller at the head of Killy's Knees to keep people from going farther, and Marty and I went back to the cornice. We gave it enough time that if someone had gotten by, which didn't seem likely because there weren't any tracks, they'd have enough time to get to the bottom. Then we started sawing. We could have saved ourselves the trouble, because the mountain started whumpfing."

I gulped down the memories, leaving only enough to come back as words for the grand jurors. Someone tried to speak, but I had to get this out in a rush or it wouldn't get out at all. I talked right over him. "And before we got the cornice a third cut through, two men skied onto the slab, and they were fighting, struggling. One of them had a gun. The other guy just wanted to get away, and he did; he just got the hell out of Dodge. I screamed at them to get off the slab, because that slide was going to happen any minute. And then, a third guy shows up, knocks the gun out of the shooter's hand, and he's trying to get off the slope. That's when I did something really stupid." I wished for a glass of water, something to fidget with, and even to drink, because I was suddenly desert-dry.

"I went out on the slab, grabbed the guy, and pulled him into the trees." Distantly I noted that the arms of the chair had sharp edges and that my knuckles were white.

"And we waited out the avalanche." The memories crowded out all the air; I couldn't pull a breath in.

"That doesn't sound stupid, that sounds brave," commented one of the jurors. She had to be a recent transplant to Colorado; the natives already knew why it was stupid. Her remark was so ludicrous it actually let me inhale again.

"It was stupid." I snorted, knowing that my reasons for pulling Jake out of harm's way might sound romantic to her. Or convince her to throw rocks, or the book, at me. I repeated, "The mountain was whumpfing."

The laughter meant someone didn't understand. "That's the sound the snowpack makes right before an avalanche. It's unstable, it's stretching and shearing; the noise sounds like 'whumpf, whumpf' and it isn't funny at all even if it is the technical term. It's the sound of disaster about to happen."

This was my big chance to convince the jurors that we hadn't killed Ulf with a set slide.

"That slide would have happened with us or without us. The cornice was still up when I stopped sawing and went after the skier, although the shaking brought it down." I could still see the toothed ribbon of the blade hanging out of the snow, the handle dangling where I abandoned it. "So yeah, going out on the slab at all was stupid. But I had to do it."

"So you rescued one of the men?" Calhoun prodded me. "What about the other?"

"He was groping around in the snow, probably for the gun, and I couldn't stop for him. The other guy was already moving. He just needed a little more speed to get clear, but the one who was down in the snow, if I'd stopped to grab him, we'd all three have been swept away. As it was, it felt really close. He got killed. We didn't."

If they wanted to know anything else, they'd have to ask. I couldn't breathe enough to talk, remembering.

"And then?" The DA gave me about a three second break to get composed.

"Marty and I got out our avalanche probes and started looking for him. We called for backup, but it still took a long time to locate him and dig him up. The snow was like cement —it always is, after a slide."

"What about the other man?" the inquisitive woman asked.

"He left; the slope was stable, and he wouldn't have been any help in the rescue. No equipment," I added, to forestall the question about how I knew this.

"And the other other guy?" she persisted. "Or will we get a nasty surprise in the spring?"

"He made it. I don't know if he took to the trees or just outran it, but the man I rescued did locate his buddy and got word to us that he had, so we didn't have to search for him. It was about the only relief that whole day." Let's see how much longer they'd go before I had to cough up names.

"What about your guard? Didn't that person see any of these people coming and head them off?" Calhoun pounded on a weak point.

"There was an injury accident on Killy's Knees and the stationed patroller was best placed to respond fast, so she wasn't there after a certain point. The cornice was already partially sawn through when she called." The guy had broken his leg in two places, we'd found out later. Allan had gotten off lightly in comparison.

"So, would you consider this entire sequence of events to be remarkably bad luck, or a planned effort, Mr. McAvoy?" Calhoun's voice was dry, and I wished he'd quit calling me by my father's name.

"It had to be bad luck, because no one part of it could have been predicted. My saw broke, we dropped the other one; it was irritating. We wanted that cornice down early in the day, and it should have happened like that. The classes were scheduled way in advance. The man who broke his leg didn't do it to lure the guard out of position. The snow storms were nature, so was the whumpfing, which didn't start until we were already at the cornice. The only one who did any evil planning was the shooter, and if that was good evil planning, he'd have lived, wouldn't he?" Getting mad was a bad idea; deep breathing calmed me down only a little.

"Ah, that reminds me...." Calhoun dug out a paper. "Did you know who the shooter was?"

"Not while he was shooting. When we dug him up I recognized him. Ulf Seiler; he was an instructor at a private ski school at Wapiti Creek. Big guy, Swiss, didn't hang much with the other ski workers. His students seemed to like him." Shut up now, Mark, you've hit the babbling stage, volunteering stuff. His students did a lot more than like him, if there were any truth to the rumors. I did know where he could take them for an afternoon of sex, but I didn't know for a fact that's what they did; they could have been drinking cocoa and playing checkers in that little cabin at the top of the mountain. Babbling, definitely babbling. I pinched the underside of my leg, and the pain helped me focus.

"Do you know of any reason why anyone would want him dead?" Oh, great. Melanie's little chickens were coming home, not just to roost but to crap in my hair.

"He was the one trying to kill someone when all this happened." I didn't think Melanie's suggestions had any merit, and I wasn't going to bring them up in an official investigation.

"Were you aware of anyone with a grudge against the late Mr. Seiler?"

"No, sir." I hadn't heard it from Mr. Underwood, only second hand from Melanie, so I wouldn't introduce hearsay. That had to be proper legal stuff, right? Hanging with Marty had some unexpected payoffs.

"No aggrieved husband of a student, say?" His voice was sharp.

"Why not an aggrieved wife? Or an aggrieved student?" I wasn't going to play the game meekly. "I didn't hang out with him—I didn't know the players in his life. I just saw him on the slopes with students."

"So, you find the string of events that put him near an avalanche to be a series of odd coincidences?" Calhoun shook his head, like he thought I was some fool for thinking it.

"I don't think him shooting at someone on a slope closed for avalanche danger was a coincidence, but Ulf had to have planned that part. The only plotting I saw going on was Ulf's." I was getting mad again. This guy had tried to kill Kurt. "And if the snow conditions plan had held, the avalanche would have happened the next day. It's not like you can point an avalanche like a gun. It might have hidden a body, but it would have been really unpredictable for killing anyone. The only person trying to kill anyone was Ulf."

"Indeed." He tapped his fingers against the wooden table he leaned against. "About that. Do you know why he was trying to kill that man?"

"Because Ulf wanted him dead?" Down, Mark, don't "duh" an irritated DA. "No, I don't. I wasn't privy to any of his thoughts."

"Never mind, that was asking for speculation. This is People's exhibit number one, the autopsy and coroner's report for Ulf Seiler." He handed a file to the court reporter. "So, you're telling me that Ulf's death was an unfortunate accident?"

"As best I can tell, yes."

"So no one suggested to you that you should arrange matters to put Ulf and danger together?"

"No."

"Or that various accidents and incidents could have been arranged, which you had no reason to suspect, which would put Ulf and peril together?" Calhoun was pacing now. It didn't look like courtroom drama, he looked genuinely agitated, and then he jerked around to stare at me when I blew his thoughts away.

"Actually, someone did suggest that." The truth, the whole truth, and nothing but the truth. See how he liked it.

"That is contradicting everything else you've just said, Mr. McAvoy. Perjury does apply in grand jury matters." His eyes flashed.

"It doesn't contradict anything, because you've been asking me about things that happened in November, until just now." Righteous indignation flooded me with heat. "In the last week, I've been approached twice about telling you that things happened just that way. They didn't, and I wasn't going to say that they did. But someone sure wanted it to look like that." I was half out of my seat with fury, and only his approach put my butt back on the chair.

"You've been remarkably sparing with names, Mr. McAvoy. Who approached you?"

"Melanie Underwood." And with that, I found myself telling the story of the chairlift rides. I tried leaving some of the ugly bits out. These people didn't need to know.

Guess they did, and Mr. Calhoun caught me at it. "Mr. McAvoy, may I remind you you're under oath?"

How long it would take the gossip to get completely around the county? It was too juicy; oaths of secrecy might not hold. They got to hear everything, even the words that got me suspended, and I felt vaguely like a traitor.

"So you hold to your theory that no one, even someone who could affect how the resort is run, influenced you in the matter of setting this avalanche." He finished up with a flourish.

"I do. Not even James Underwood can make the mountain whumpf on cue." I wasn't going to dance around the man's name. If Calhoun wanted to pretend that I didn't know who he meant was pulling my strings, I wouldn't help.

"It seems to me that the only persons who might shed any

more light on this are the man who was being shot at and the one who knocked the gun away." All the adrenaline left me at once. "Do you know who they were?"

The talk from the potluck, which seemed a million years ago now, buzzed in my head. "Don't lie to the grand jury," Kurt had advised me. "We'll handle it." I hoped they could. I hoped he meant it, because I was going to take his advice.

"Kurt Carlson and Jake Landon. They work at Wapiti Creek." In the funk of having given up friends, I barely registered the thanks for my testimony.

One last question rang out—surely it wasn't part of the proceedings. "Mr. McAvoy? Did you want to save Ulf?" It was the inquisitive juror, and she ignored the DA's attempt to hush her.

"Yes."

The court reporter still typed away, recording her next question, which seemed like genuine concern. "How do you feel about not saving Ulf? Are you okay?"

"No, I'm not okay." I looked her full in the face. "And he haunts my dreams."

NINETEEN

The bailiff led me back to Marty and Allan, and I was never so glad to see friendly faces. I wished we could go home, but the bailiff led Marty off to the courtroom and I found the comfort of Allan's hand. After nearly three days, or forty-five minutes by the clock, Marty returned. "Let's get out of here."

Thirty-six or so hours without much sleep and all the stress had made me shaky, but it was the opportunity to walk out of that courthouse free that really put the wobble in my step.

Allan noticed. "Let Marty drive." I handed over the keys without a murmur, having already figured out that I could drag the crate over to the passenger side and stick my arm through to the front seat and drape it over Allan. My arm was sort of asleep before we got halfway back to Wapiti Creek, but it was worth it.

"See? Not so bad as you'd feared." Marty took the curvy road with enough caution not to slide me around the back.

"Let's see what Kurt and Jake think once they've had a chance to visit with Mr. Calhoun." The yawn cut my last word in two.

"They were more sinned against than sinning," Marty

remarked. "Jake did nothing besides prevent a murder, and if Ulf hadn't stopped to grope for the gun, he could have gotten away."

Even in my exhaustion, I could detect something weird. "Now you're talking about it? When you wouldn't before?" Anger tinged the words, making Allan squeeze my nearly numb fingers.

"Rules in Colorado are different," Marty replied sheepishly. "I asked. First Amendment and all. It's the grand jurors who can't talk about anything they've learned in there."

"Remind me to slip you some decaf one cold early morning." All the coffee in the world couldn't have kept me from dozing off the last few miles.

"See you for dinner, guys." Marty handed Allan the keys. How'd we get to the back of the restaurant kitchen so fast?

"Yeah. See you." Allan unlatched the sliding door for me. "Mark, are you okay?"

I slid out of the van and nearly went to my knees on the pavement. "Nothing that a good night's sleep won't put right. Didn't get much last night."

He put his good arm out to steady me. "Did you get any at all?"

"Uh, no. Let's get the chow delivered and everyone fed." I made it up the two steps to the door without falling. The warmth of the kitchen contrasted with the cold outdoors, and the air was full of good smells, making my stomach rumble in appreciation. I hadn't eaten much today, either. Kurt and Gabe looked up from the computer screen to greet us.

"You aren't doing any of that. You're a wreck." Allan would have to say that in front of Kurt. Jeez. "Hi, guys. I'll be with you in a sec. Come on, Mark."

He crutched out of the kitchen and back to the bar area,

where the dustcover lay tangled on the couch. "Please, don't argue. You're wiped. Penny, Kurt, and I can get the deliveries run pretty fast, and you catch some Zs on the couch."

"I can help," I insisted stubbornly, but the couch did look inviting.

"You could, but then when we go to bed early, you'll go to sleep, and what if I want to be awake a little longer?" He put his arms around me, warm and solid. "A nap now will make staying awake for me later a lot more fun," he offered.

His wet tongue stroking over my lip and stealing into my mouth convinced me alertness later was in my best interest. "You have a point."

I think I was out cold before he pulled the dust sheet all the way to my shoulders.

Allan and Kurt came back to retrieve me, Gabe, and food for the kitchen crew. The ride back to the apartment building was a jabber of computer terms. Gabe outlined his afternoon's efforts. "The dropdown menus load to a form that talks to the Excel spreadsheet, which should...." I couldn't keep track, but Gabe sounded pleased, and if it made Allan's life easier, that was a good thing, because maybe then he wouldn't have to keep dragging the phone out of his pocket. It rang again before we got upstairs.

The turnout tonight was just about the whole gang, even if they weren't kitchen crew, because everyone wanted to know about the grand jury. "I just gave them the brief rundown on what happened and why we ended up triggering late." Everyone pretty much knew all that. "What did you tell them, Marty?"

"Some of that, but they seemed more interested in you. How I know you, why I work with you. How much I trust you. It was weird, really. And they wanted to know about Alpenschlössl." He looked over at Kurt and Jake, who sat cross-legged on the floor with their bowls of ragout and carrots. "They wanted everything I knew about Rudi. And they asked who the mystery men were."

"They did. Point-blank." I tried to apologize with my eyes.

"I told you: we'll handle it." Kurt glanced over to Jake. Silent communication flowed between them; they said more with a look than I could manage with a dictionary.

"The one who's going to have the biggest issue from all this is Rudi," Jake told him. "He's going to think you reneged on keeping quiet about his little scheme."

"Probably, even if we don't tell them anything incriminating." Kurt bit his next forkful as though he wished it was Rudi's head, and chewed. "How much would you bet he can make it all sound like naughty, dead Ulf's fault?"

"They aren't going to arrest him on nothing but your word, even if you told them a million lurid things," Marty pointed out. "They'll investigate, find evidence."

"If it's the law and not the media swooping in, he may not connect it to us." Kurt dropped his fork with a clatter in his empty dish.

"They run it so smoothly that it doesn't look like a sex business, so why would it even come up?" Kim took her plate and Kurt's to the kitchen.

"Because the whole reason I went to the top of the mountain after Ulf is because I thought he had Jake and was going to do something awful, and the only reason Jake followed us is that he knew Ulf had threatened to do that. Follow the string of 'why' and the sex comes up," Kurt griped.

"If Rudi treats it like it was Ulf's little sideline, he's clear," Kim pointed out. "And you're clear. And if the DA really wants to pursue Rudi, he'll have to investigate and get fresh, unconnected-with-you evidence."

"The only thing that connects you to the grand jury is the rumor mill, so if we keep quiet, you guys go in, testify, and get out, no issues. They don't release grand jury testimony," Marty put in. At a sharp look from me, he added, "Even in Colorado. I asked."

"I have to tell Charlie I need the time off. Try keeping a secret from him." Kurt had Charlie's number, all right.

"There's nothing Charlie likes better than being in the know, and, Kurt, he doesn't blab indiscriminately, if it's important and you ask him not to." We all turned to Julie, who hadn't said much this entire meal. She blushed. "Well, he doesn't. Tell him what's going on, why it's important that only he know it, and he won't spread it around."

"So, girlfriend, what's this big secret that you've been keeping from all of us?" Kim pounced. She, Julie, and Chelsea had been buddies for three years, so if Kim didn't know, it was a well-kept secret indeed.

"If I wanted everyone to know, I would have told you myself." Julie looked sorry she'd mentioned anything at all, and got up off the carpet. "Good night. Thanks for dinner. It was good." She paused on the way out the door to kiss Allan's cheek.

"I have good kitchen staff," he told her, tweaking her long braid, and she did laugh just a tiny bit.

Gabe followed her to the door, but stopped and turned to Allan. "I need another couple of hours with the website, and it should be fully functional. I have all the fill-in fields invisible right now, so it isn't making promises it can't fulfill. Maybe tomorrow evening I could go over and work on it?"

"Sure!" Allan's phone rang again, and after that, I would have been willing to pick the lock on the kitchen just to let Gabe in to the computer.

Everyone left in the next few minutes, leaving us with a

counter littered with bowls that had migrated from Allan's kitchen to mine, a handful of dirty silverware, and a pan all but licked clean. I ran a sink of soapy water. Weird ripping noises penetrated the sound of the running water.

"What are you doing?"

The lone chair had been Allan's by right of injury, and now he sat pulling Velcro fastenings apart. "I'm going to take the braces off for a while. Don't worry, I won't try to walk on it, but the worst is over; I can start going without for a while. It will be good for my range of motion." He dropped the leg brace beside the chair and set his foot on the carpet. "Mmm. Feels good!"

"Are you sure you should be doing that?"

He'd started ripping open the arm brace.

"Sure, I'm sure. Why not?" He flexed his hand experimentally. "Mark, I'm not lifting anything, I'm not walking around —it's okay. The doc said so. Don't look so worried."

I was worried. What if he did lift something? What if he tried walking and the injury got worse? I wouldn't let him overdo it.

"Come here." Allan motioned me to him, and I knelt between his knees to put my arms around him and lay my head on his chest. He held me close, speaking quietly. "The ligaments are healing, okay? It's not a big deal. I don't hurt, and the joints shouldn't be immobilized for long periods or it causes other problems. Quit worrying so much." I snuggled closer, and he rubbed his cheek in my hair. "You aren't convinced, are you?"

I shook my head silently. Nope, not convinced at all.

"You have to know about these sorts of injuries, right? Patrollers have to know, I thought."

I nodded. His sprains were surely worse than anyone else's.

"Then relax and let me feel the pleasure of not being strapped together, okay? Nothing's going to happen." He stroked my back, and it had to be his unbraced left hand. "You're such a worrywart."

"I do worry about you." Mumbled into his chest, the words were still audible. He groaned.

"Tell you what, how about I promise to play with your cock with only my right hand tonight?" Allan laughed, but it sounded like a really good idea. "Will that make you stop worrying?"

"Depends on how good you play with it." Kissing him kept any more fussy things from coming out of my mouth. I could tell I was irritating him, but.... Couldn't he see how much I cared? "And when do you plan to start?"

"Oh, pretty soon now." He pulled my turtleneck out of my waistband and started stroking my skin. "Let's get this off." He was using that hand again. I yanked on the turtleneck and didn't quite pull an ear off. "Nice start."

His dress shirt unbuttoned easily enough, and we wiggled him out of his trousers, though I started to growl when he stood up to drop them from his hips. "Chill, Mark." He sat back down and that put him in sucking range.

He wasn't going to try to get out of that chair again anytime soon, not with the way I was licking and nibbling on him. Allan's cock stood straight up, poking my chin with each damp caress I bestowed over his belly and chest. To tease, I'd slip the head briefly into my mouth, then find something else to do. When I got to his balls, Allan wove his fingers into my hair to keep my mouth from wandering off. "There, yeah, like that. Oh...." Keeping those sounds going meant sliding him in and out of my mouth, first one ball, then the other, and then sucking both in where I could roll them over my tongue. His sack was slightly scratchy, not quite smooth any more, making me wonder how often he depilated. Who'd think a hot kitchen could provide such a nice benefit for sex? I flicked my tongue between his balls, stroking them both.

"I can't reach you," he eventually complained, though not until after I'd decided to suck on his cock, until he stopped me and pinched the base firmly for a moment. "I wanna throw you down on the bed."

"No walking!" Allan had gotten to his feet, but he wasn't going anywhere on that ankle. Nipping at his neck let me figure out how I'd transport him. My arms under his ass let him wrap his legs around my waist again, and again we fell together to the protesting mattress. With every step, my cock had rubbed against his crack; I'd just keep on going. A little rubber, a little lube, I'd be in.

Allan had other ideas. "Come up here!" The man was strong; he nearly lifted me where he wanted me, which was straddling his head. Always good. I fucked his mouth slowly, knowing his other end would still be there after the sensuous attentions from his mouth. Good to his word, he held me with his right hand, letting the left roam over my butt.

"Hey! Should you be doing that?" I whipped around after doing a quick hand inventory; he'd taken both hands away for a moment, and now he was pumping my cock with the right.

"Not if you don't like it." Allan withdrew the slick finger from my hole.

"I like it—it's just—that's your left hand." I didn't know what to do. I wanted that finger back, but not if it would reinjure him.

"It's not like I'm getting a lot of wrist action here, Mark. Not like whacking off." He slipped in again, very slowly. "So if you like it, I'm going to keep doing it, and after a while I'm going to do it with my cock." He slid out, then back, turning my brain to "low."

"Uh, okay. As long as you—"

"Yeah, yeah, don't hurt myself. Chill, Mark." He put my cock back in his mouth and encouraged me to slide between his tongue and his finger. Maybe I should just chill and let him do what he wanted. Oh yeah…

"Where's a condom?"

Damn. I had to disengage from his mouth to fish one out of the side drawer, so I knelt next to him, rolling it on and knowing I'd be back on top in a moment. Allan tried to sit up and grab the lube, but I pushed him back down and squished some on. That little cranky look went away really fast as I stroked him slippery. I'd make it really good so he wouldn't keep trying to use that hand.

"Don't get up, Allan." Collecting a kiss and throwing a leg over him gave me a minute to relax and get ready for something I hadn't done in a long time and hoped I'd had enough preparation for. Ready, aim, slide, and the burn told me to take him in slowly enough to stretch. He coaxed me down over him until I could sit firmly on his hips, adjusting to the unfamiliar fullness that somehow made my chest hollow at the same time.

"Take your time, Mark," he told me, his hands firmly on my thighs, not urging me to move.

Running my hands over his chest and belly gave me something else to think about while the discomfort became pleasure. There was some give to Allan's flesh, solid and warm as he was, and I pushed against him to feel it, and then I had to push against him with the rest of me. Slowly at first, then more wildly, slowing once to lean down for a kiss that became a tangle of wet tongues and a lick in the cleft of his chin. He wiped away the wetness with his left hand, because he'd wrapped that strong right hand around my cock. My world got very small as we fucked each other, about the size of our bodies, and then it exploded into drops of come and waves of pleasure that crashed through me every time Allan thrust, racing to his own explosion.

Swaying slightly, I watched his chest heave in the aftermath, his eyes nearly closed. He was so gloriously alive after that orgasm. I put both hands against his torso just to feel him breathe, much as I'd done with—never mind. Allan was the only man who mattered here.

TWENTY

"I'll get your brace and crutches." I pulled Allan back onto the bed. "Stay."

"One or the other; I don't need both!" he grumped, but he was doing exactly what I'd been afraid of. Last night the bathroom trip had been accomplished with his arm over my shoulder, at my insistence, and he'd very pointedly aimed his penis at the toilet using his left hand. I hadn't said anything then, but this was too much.

"Which do you want?" I brandished both at him.

"The crutch. Then I can both hobble around and *klopp* you with it. Mark!" Allan grabbed the brace out of my hand and strapped his foot into it. "I'm healing. You're overprotective. It's annoying, so stop it." He ignored me when I tried to give him a hand off the bed.

"You're walking on that ankle!"

"Yes, I am, and I'm going to do it for a while. 'Weight bearing as tolerated.' We'll see how I tolerate it." Allan put his arms around my waist. "It's weird. No one has carried me in maybe twenty-six or twenty-seven years, and you've done it three times in the last few days." He nibbled my lip, which toned down my worry not at all. "Don't do that again."

"You needed me to do that." Didn't he appreciate that I was taking care of him?

"I did then, but not now." His left hand rubbed up and down my back, to make a point, no doubt. "It makes me feel helpless, or like a little kid."

"Not even in the throes of caveman lust?" I looked for loopholes, because I could tell he was revving up to overdo it.

"Check back with me on that one, after the brace has been off for a couple weeks. Feeling like a kid is not sexy. I like it on equal terms, and, Mark—" Allan looked me straight in the eye and then met my lips hard but briefly. "Sometimes I like to be the one directing traffic in bed."

"I'll remember that." I put my mouth to his more softly, wanting to promise him anything that would keep him from letting go.

"I need to get to the kitchen before the food truck gets there."

"*We* need to get there," I reminded him. "I'm kitchen staff again."

"Thought today I had Jake and Chelsea." Allan started hobbling around after his clothes, ignoring the crutches I held out.

"Yes, but I'm not working today. I can help, too." His other brace was on the floor by the chair, so I brought it and his clothes.

"Or you can do the stuff you'd normally do on your day off. I think the three of us can manage okay. Look, my arm is a lot better." He flexed his wrist for me.

"Stop that!" I started to pop the brace on him. "I'm kitchen staff."

"Mark...." I hadn't heard Allan growl before. "If you're going to be a pain, you aren't kitchen staff."

"Okay, I'll stop." If it meant he'd make me stay home, I'd just watch, intervene as needed, and hope I wasn't too late.

"Good. Get in the shower. I'll see you at the van." He kissed me once more and hobbled back to his place, leaving me staring stupidly at the wrist brace in my hand.

"Good morning, Charlie." James Underwood wondered what kind of news he'd phone in today. So far this week, Charlie, while being a fountain of information both directly and indirectly, hadn't said anything that made Underwood happy. The next bit was more of the same.

"Do you want me to schedule a different instructor for the kids today, or did you want me to shuffle Kurt's schedule for tomorrow?" Charlie asked. "It seems he needs to be in Phippsburg this afternoon, at Simon Calhoun's request."

"Did he get a subpoena, too?" Underwood rubbed a hand over his face.

"He and Jake Landon both did, but they tagged Jake for a day off, poor fella. Oh, and Jake sends his apologies to the kids that he can't ski with them after the lesson." Charlie chuckled. "Calhoun might even want to talk to Rudi Gernsbach, since he was Ulf's boss. Haven't heard about that, though."

Ah, yes, Rudi. Underwood reflected that he hadn't decided what to do about Alpenschlössl. Tossing the ski school to Simon Calhoun would be satisfying for the whole three minutes before the press turned it into a snowy sex scandal with his wife's name at the top of the list. There had to be another way.

Once he concluded the call with Charlie, Underwood

reached for a topographical map of the ski area. It butted up against federal land, marked in green, and the Alpenschlössl cabin should be right about here.... Underwood ran a finger along the map and hummed a little tune.

Allan held out the keys to me once I got to the parking lot, saying nothing but accepting the brace and watching me put the crutches in the back of the van. Jake and Chelsea peeked in the back, raised eyebrows at the plastic crate, and then Jake produced his own keys.

"I think I'll drive us. Kurt and I need to be in Phippsburg this afternoon, so the wheels will help. See you in a few minutes." He and Chelsea left, snickering about crosshatch patterns on butts.

"They must have gotten served last night," I commented. "Didn't take Calhoun long to send out the minion."

"Who probably had instructions to be swift this time or risk the wrath of Simon," Allan added.

I wasn't risking further wrath of Allan; I drove without a single comment about the brace, which he hadn't put on. It had the feeling of a test, one I was determined to pass.

We able-bodied crew humped in cases and crates from the delivery truck, and then sat down to prep vegetables under Allan's watchful eye. I was entrusted with a knife again, and I made sure that I didn't take my feelings out on the food or my own flesh. Of course, this time it was frustration, once we'd chopped enough onions to make the whole world cry and Allan started to sauté them in batches. Chelsea heated a couple of pans while Jake and I worked on reducing very large chunks of beef to bite-sized morsels.

"Stirring works, but it breaks up the pieces. Do it like this," Allan instructed her, and shook the big pan in a circular motion that flipped everything over. "Same thing with the pine nuts." He'd started toasting those in a skillet as well.

"Hey!" burst out of my mouth before I thought. "Don't pick that up!"

He turned very slowly toward me. "Mark, relax. The brace is on, and I didn't pick both pans up like I usually do." Allan glowered at me a moment and then went back to coaching Chelsea. "Give it a flip." She used both hands and the pine nuts showered around.

"Guess it's a skill," she marveled, and tried again, keeping most of the nuts in the pan this time.

"It is. Keep the onions moving, too. It isn't just a TV chef trick." Allan came to inspect the large mounds of bloody beef Jake and I were dissecting. "Jake, give me a hand in the walk-in."

I would have done it, and groped his ass while we were in there, which probably explained why he asked Jake. I'd just annoyed him again, and Chelsea called me on it while they were out of earshot.

"Trust him, Mark. He's probably hurt himself often enough to know about getting reinjured. Randi told me that chefs damage themselves fairly often." She tried flipping the food again, using both hands on the pan and turning it without the deftness he'd shown. "Have you been treating him like that since he got hurt?"

"I'm just trying to take care of him!" I protested.

"No wonder he's cranky." She struggled with the other pan. "Keep chopping meat like that, and you'll get busted back to potato peel duty again." Julie had ratted me out at dinner the night before. I took another look at what I was doing and tried to keep the pieces more even. She glanced up at the walk-in. The door was still closed. "Back off a little. He's a grown man, and he didn't even know you a week ago."

I just grunted something non-committal. She didn't have to remind me of that.

Jake and Allan reappeared with more things to be peeled, chopped, diced, seared, and otherwise turned into food that none of us could have made unsupervised. By the time we put everything including the macaroni and cheese into the ovens, Jake had only cleared his throat at me once, and Chelsea had said, "Ah!" once, as though I were a dog getting trained, but Allan hadn't told me off again. Instead, he'd smiled at me when I lifted the sixty-five quart stockpot, which did have to weigh a hundred pounds, and it wasn't near full.

"Thanks, guys," he said, adding chips and pickles to the plates with the giant turkey sandwiches we made for our own lunch. "This will be good."

"I think I've eaten one of these before," Jake said, eyeing the thick sandwich. "Do you cater Alpenschlössl?"

"Yes, a couple lunches a few times a week. Why?" Allan took a bite of his own sandwich, less lavishly stacked than Jake's or mine.

"It's just that they're going to be in trouble after today, I think." Jake looked at him ruefully. "The DA is probably going to ask questions that will put Rudi under the bus."

"Clients come and clients go," Allan muttered philosophically. "The Underwoods are now two separate clients, so no net difference, I guess." He glanced at me, which turned my insides to marshmallow and my cock to wood. I wanted to lay him down on the prep table right there.

"Hey, I have to run. I need to change and collect Kurt. Wish us luck." Jake left to a ragged chorus of good wishes. He and Kurt would have all sorts of interesting questions to answer this afternoon. I just hoped that there would be no major fallout for them. Chelsea left with him, and that left the two of us alone in the warm kitchen.

"What's on the agenda for this afternoon?" I waggled my eyebrows seductively.

"How about some smooching before I hit the paperwork?" Allan waggled his own eyebrows. "I need to collate tickets and put in a food order. Some things, alas, can't be delegated."

"Some things shouldn't be delegated." I kissed him softly but thoroughly, with one hand on the back of his head. "Except let's delegate us to the couch."

We hadn't gotten to the serious, clothes-off stage of the kissing when Allan's phone went off. "Business," he said apologetically, fishing the phone from a pocket. I held him against my chest while he took the call, but it was short and not food-related. "Oh, that's right, you do. I'd forgotten. Thanks."

After he hung up, he leaned his head on my shoulder. "In all the excitement, I forgot I left my ski boot at the clinic. They just called to remind me."

"Shall we go collect it?" I dragged lazy fingers up and down his spine. "Or should I go and you do your paperwork?"

"Would you? That mountain isn't going to get smaller for being ignored." He sighed, and I silently agreed: his desk was a mess.

"No problem." I hated paperwork; this way, I could do something for him and avoid doing any myself. He snuggled tighter against me, and we went back to brushing our lips over each other's faces. "I suppose we should save the heavy-duty smooching for later if we're going to get things done, huh?"

"Probably." But neither of us was in a big hurry to break off what we were doing.

The next time I came up for air, I had to ask. "Allan?"

"Mmmm?" His lips were against my neck.

"Is it okay if I love you just a little bit?"

He froze, and then he stopped nuzzling me. "Um, no." His voice was soft, almost apologetic, and sounded more like he should have been saying "yes."

It was still a knife to my heart. "Because?" My voice was equally soft, though I wanted to yell out.

"We don't know each other well enough, Mark. It's been only a few days, and we've hardly been together when someone isn't hurt or scared. We don't know what 'normal' is for each other." He was scared? He couldn't mean me.

"I think we've gotten to know each other pretty well." Brushing my lips across his forehead, I tried to make my case.

"Where did I grow up, and how does my family think of me being gay?" He made his case with greater detail, damn it. "What's my middle name, Mark?"

"What is your middle name? Mine's Thomas." One less possible objection.

"Vencel, but there's a story behind it, and that's the sort of thing we don't know about each other. How can you know so fast, Mark?" He looked me straight in the eye.

"Well.... Just the way I feel about you?" Vencel?

"You're hornier than hell for me, and that's great, because I'm hornier than hell for you, too. But, Mark?" He kissed the corner of my mouth. "Don't you think you should find out whether I like milk chocolate or dark chocolate better before you decide you love me?"

"Which do you like better?" He couldn't wiggle out of this that easily.

"That's the sort of thing you find out by being with me. So

—" he interrupted himself to kiss me again. "Let's just keep finding these things out as we go, okay?"

At least it was a qualified no, and I'd turn it into a yes soon enough. "Okay. I can find out what size shoes you wear by collecting your ski boot."

He laughed. "See? We learn each other with time. And if I don't get my billing done, we learn how broke I'm going to be." Allan got up from the couch and pulled me to standing close enough for a full body rub. "I'll get this finished and then we can do deliveries. Bring the van back in one piece, please."

I left him at the desk, sorting papers, and headed to the hospital in Phippsburg. Maybe that would be my last stop, since I now had some other errands to run. I'd keep my feelings to myself for the time being, but it didn't change what I felt. He'd be okay alone for a while. How much mischief could he get into?

The answer was "plenty." I got back with the ski boot, the paperwork the clinic had tucked into it, and a goodie bag of treats to help me get to know him better, to find a locked kitchen and a note saying "at apartment, back at four thirty." He must have hopped the shuttle, so I drove back to employee housing, wondering if he'd gotten everything done. Taking the stairs two at a time with his boot, my bag, and his crutches got me to the third floor in time to see Allan dragging a plastic laundry basket down the hall like a balky puppy, leashed with a belt.

"What are you doing?" Throwing the boot and the bag on top of the laundry, I grabbed the basket. "I'll get this."

"I've got it, Mark." Allan didn't let go of the belt, nor did he take the crutches. "Mark. I've got it."

"I'll do it." I was irritated with him. Why didn't he wait for me to do this sort of thing? His door was unlocked, so I brought the basket, which he'd finally relinquished, in to dump on the couch for folding. "You shouldn't be doing this, Allan. Your wrist isn't that much better."

"I wasn't carrying anything, Mark, and it isn't that damaged, either. This is really pissing me off." Allan was growling again. "I can do most of what I need to do even braced up; you're acting like I'm some little fragile thing that needs total looking after, and it's gotten massively irritating. Knock. It. Off."

"Hey, I just want to take care of you while you're hurt!" How could he be so angry?

"I'm not that hurt! Mark, I am thirty-one years old, I can take care of most everything, and you've been hovering like some horny helicopter. It isn't that I don't appreciate what you've done, it's that you keep doing it after I don't need it any longer!" The growl had gone to a shout. "You're under a lot of stress, I get that, but I haven't quit being a grown man!"

"You needed me to go get your boot." None of this was making sense.

"No, I could have fetched the boot myself, or called Kurt or Jake. They were already in Phippsburg. I asked you just to get you out of my hair for a while without hurting your feelings." My jaw dropped and so did the volume of his voice.

"Mark, this is one of those things that you don't know me well enough to understand without being told, but I am used to being alone a lot." Now he sounded gentle, almost consoling. "I am good company for myself; I am used to it. And you and I have been together constantly, I mean *constantly*, since I got back from the hospital. Like, every single minute. You don't even like it if I go to the bathroom by myself. I need some breathing room, damn it." The volume had risen again.

"I thought you liked being with me. You said you were horny for me."

"I do like being with you, mostly, except for the overdone hovering, and I am horny for you. I just thought that being joined at the hip was during sex. Not all the damned time, and not when you don't listen when I ask you to back off. But damn, I'm feeling smothered here, and then you ask if you can love me a little and if I say yes, how do you act then? More of this?" He sat down next to the laundry basket with a flop.

"I just wanted…." What else could I say?

"To take care of me. I know." He put his head in his hands and rubbed his scalp. "But this is what I meant when I said we hadn't seen each other normal yet. I've been hurt, and you've had your regular life screwed up beyond belief." He looked back up at me. "So I'm trying to be understanding, but you're making me fucking crazy."

"I… I'm sorry. I…." Words choked me, feelings choked me. "I just want to get between you and anything that might hurt you." My palm came first to his shoulder and then to his head, where his hair rasped my skin for what might be the last time. "Now I'm the thing that hurts you." A kiss from the crazy man might be the last thing he wanted, but I pressed my lips to his head all the same, and then I fled.

TWENTY-ONE

Dinner was tense. I'd almost put a sign on the door directing everyone to Allan's place, but stopped, not wanting to splash my misery around on everyone else, not wanting them to know. Kurt and Jake kept up most of the conversation, telling about their grand jury experiences.

"If the DA doesn't go after Rudi, I'd be surprised," Kurt finished. "I'm just very glad that the questions revolved around what happened on the mountain."

"That could change," Jake said darkly. "We're supposed to go back."

Allan and I had barely spoken beyond the needs of getting dinner, and I sat next to him to eat only because everyone left that spot open and there wasn't really another, short of hiding in the kitchen. He let me refill his glass once, only because I was already up when I asked, but I stayed out of his way as he dished himself a plate, and didn't fight to carry it, even though he was using one crutch to get around. The fight was with myself—I wanted to take it so badly that I succeeded in dumping over my own plate and spent the next few minutes cleaning sauce out of the carpet while he limped over to the easy chair.

Would he stay? I didn't know and wouldn't ask. What if that made him feel smothered? A trip to the dumpster let me escape during cleanup. I stayed outside and watched the clouds scud over the stars until I was frozen, and went back to a quiet and empty apartment. My body warmed slowly, and my soul was still icy when I woke alone, heart pounding and the echo of my scream in my head. Sleep didn't come back after the nightmare, and the pillow I clutched until dawn was no substitute for Allan.

Morning brought another problem. I wasn't scheduled kitchen crew, but I'd been there every day. Did he expect me to be there, need the help? When I caught him at the van, we had an audience. Devon sat in the driver's seat, damn him, and Julie on the crate.

"Need another set of hands?" I asked through the window he'd rolled down.

"Need, no. I'm doing pretty good, but if you want to...." That was not a ringing invitation. "You've been kitchen help every single day without a break. Isn't there something you'd do on a day off?" Allan looked at me, and I didn't know what to make of what was in his eyes.

"I haven't been skiing since...." If he could do without me in the kitchen, I'd do something he hadn't a prayer of doing at my level.

"Go skiing then. Have some fun." His mouth quirked, as if he'd caught the thought. "Work up an appetite for dinner."

I didn't, though; I went back upstairs and threw myself on a bed that still smelled faintly of him. Ripping off the sheets and stuffing them into the washer would only make the scent go away, not the memories. This had to be a record even for me;

fall in love, take five days from first kiss to last. Every random encounter with tourists was shorter, but that was sex, not love. What was between me and Allan, even if he wouldn't call it love, was supposed to last.

I remade the bed with fresh sheets and ignored the knocking at the door. The phone tweeted and I turned it off, not checking. As far as I knew, Allan still didn't have my number. Why would he? We'd been together all the time.

The knocking disturbed me again a few hours later, rousing me from the stupor I'd fallen into on the easy chair. A glance at the clock told me Allan would still be busy cooking now. We hadn't finished as early as eleven any day this week. So I ignored it.

After ten minutes of silence I went to collect the dry sheets, and came back to more knocking, which was really strange, because I'd just entered through the front door.

"Mark, you asshole, let me in! Right now!" Thuds of angry woman beating on glass took a moment to register, and it really didn't seem safe to let an apoplectic Kim come in from the little balcony. "I know you're in there!"

"What the hell?" It would probably be less safe to leave her out there: she might come right through the glass. Which neighbor had let her out to do a Spider-Man imitation on the balconies? No wonder she was so mad.

"Took you long enough!" She glowered at me, ripping the headband away from her brown mop. "Mark, what exactly do you think you're doing?" She unzipped her burgundy jacket, just like the one I didn't have now.

"Giving Allan some space. It's what he wanted." Why was I explaining to the Super-meddler? "And what makes it your business?"

"You're a friend, and you're being a jerk. Giving Allan some space, fine, but you're sitting around moping. Your life hasn't stopped completely. You were a zombie last night at dinner, and you said you were going skiing today, and here you are—" She gave the laundry basket a contemptuous kick, as if I hadn't accomplished anything. How'd she know that? Oh, yeah, from Julie to Kim, and maybe three other people as Kim worked out that I hadn't been on the mountain; no one had scanned my lift ticket.

"He wants you to go have some fun, and you're doing laundry?" She picked up my clean sheets and let them drop back into the basket. "Oh, and doing 'woe is me' laundry, too. Geez, Mark!"

"Don't you think you've interfered enough? And he just wants me to do anything that isn't hovering around him. Laundry is as good as skiing or fetching a ski boot for that." I shook my head. "I really screwed up."

"It might not be that big a screwup, Mark." Kim quit yelling and put her arms around me. "It can still be okay. You guys haven't really talked, have you?"

Cold comfort. "We talked enough. He called me a helicopter and said I was driving him fucking crazy," I admitted into her hair, wishing she was Allan.

"Well, then stop with the helicopter and get back to the fucking." She grinned up at me. "Show him the real Mark, not this Hovering Harry! He'll like you better that way. Go, get dressed and come back to the mountain with me. I am not taking 'no' for an answer."

Laundry had been the trigger for our fight yesterday, I recalled, pulling on the polypropylene long johns. The bag I'd thrown on top of Allan's clothing had been meant to get us to talk, to solve some of his objections to me loving him. It contained two chocolate bars—one milk, one dark—and I'd wanted us to eat them as he told me the story of that odd middle name. If Kim was right, I might find out yet. And in the meantime, I could ski Wapiti Creek like a tourist. It could all be a lot worse.

"I gotta get back to work, Mark." Kim smacked my arm once we'd offloaded at the top of the Upper Scott lift. "Go play in the slalom gates on Hotdog Bun." She sailed off the other way, toward Killy's Knees, where trouble often lurked, possibly in the form of that semi-tanked celebrity snowboarder and his Hawaiian-patterned buddy. Cal and pal had gotten off the lift about four chairs ahead of us. I wasn't patrolling, so they weren't my problem, but old habits and memory both lingered; I noticed where they went. Kim could manage, and I had no desire to talk to him. He wasn't half the equal of the man who'd... just thrown me out. I poled off to check out some slalom gates.

The gates were in use when I got there. A whole bunch of blue-and-white-jacketed men waited turns to pound through them. Jorey waved me to a stop, though the others didn't give me more than brief nods once they noticed I wasn't a fellow ski team member.

"You're actually practicing with the team?" I had to twit the rebel for being so conventional.

"For a while, just to be sure they remember who I am," Jorey told me, teeth flashing white as the snow under his feet. "It makes victory so much sweeter. What's with the blue jacket? You aren't patrolling?"

Not wanting to explain my involuntary days off, I just shrugged. "I'm allowed a good time." I studied a racer's form as he whipped through the gates and shot down the hill. Damn.

"Always a good time around here!" Jorey thumped my back,

nearly knocking me off my skis. "You get lucky the other night?"

I wasn't going to discuss Allan with him. "See you later, Jorey." I bypassed the gates on my way down, and it wasn't a particular shock when he caught up and passed me in a few minutes, only to wait for me at the bottom of the lift.

"Hey, sorry, man. I didn't either, but you can always hope, right?" His smile was infectious; I did have to respond a little.

"Dumbass, you were hitting on the ones that were taken."

"They aren't always permanently taken when I start hitting on them." He craned his neck. "Now, there's one that's taken, but she's a major MILF." I looked where he was looking, and damn, if it wasn't Melanie Underwood. She and her kids were farther ahead in the lift line, chatting with Cal the action hero and his stooge. "Single! Hey, Melanie! I'm single for you!"

She motioned at him with a smile, showing no sign of having seen me, and I was alone in the lift line, loading with strangers. Jorey had his arm over Melanie's shoulder before I had the safety bar down, which made me look for Gracie and Todd. There they were, sitting with the action hero, two chairs ahead of their mother.

Not my problem, I reminded myself, but still couldn't keep that thought once I'd gotten to the top of the mountain. The only slope on the high peak the twins had any business on was the intermediate Killy's Knees. All the rest up here were black diamonds and double black diamonds. Every patroller was aware of the kids and their huge desire to hit the expert slopes: our boss and the Big Boss had both made it clear we were to prevent that. Melanie was standing and chatting with Jorey when I pulled up next to them. The twins were nowhere to be seen.

"Melanie! Jorey! Where are the kids?" Suspended or not, I

was one worried patroller. "Hey, Gabe!" I screamed for the lift attendant, glad he was a friend.

"Todd! Gracie!" Melanie called, as if I would have asked had they been in earshot. "I don't know! They rode with Cal and Pete, and now where—"

"They went that way with the movie star!" Gabe called from the offload zone. "I told the kids to do Killy's Knees, but they were talking about Cement Chute."

"Come on, we have to get them!" I swung away from Melanie and Jorey. "Come on! I can't manage them both, Jorey." Asking Gabe to abandon the lift wasn't even an option.

"Hell, yeah, I'm tired of running slalom gates anyhow." Jorey stepped sideways, away from Melanie. "Let's fetch your rugrats, sweetie, and if they're on Killy's Knees anyhow, Mark and I can race Cement Chute." He might be the coach's despair, but I was glad now for his joyous disregard of doing things with the team.

"I can't do Cement Chute," she wavered, and I knew she was right. She'd only be another casualty.

"I don't see them." We stood at the head of Killy's Knees. No small children trailed the black-and-silver snowboarder and his shadow in the Hawaiian pants. With those two, though, the kids might be leading. "Melanie, you head down and wait at the junction with Cement Chute. The kids have to be on one slope or the other. We'll find them."

We had to.

The tracks on the traverse to Cement Chute didn't tell me much about who had passed that way recently; too many were fairly fresh. "Do you really think those two clowns encouraged the kids to try the black diamonds?" Jorey was a frequent guest at the Underwoods' and knew the kids about as well as I did.

"Yeah. I think so, and you didn't help, chatting up

Mommy." I could talk with him, since we both had the skill and control to make haste and speak. "Bet she'd like to get her hooks into you."

"What?" Jorey yelped. The trees were just up ahead; we'd have to get through them to see the rest of the slope.

"They're getting divorced. She's already shopping for whoever can give her what she wants." She'd tried to buy me, the bitch. I turned through the trees. "Anyone who reads *Ski Magazine* knows how much you pull down in endorsements, and you're better looking than Ulf." We got through the trees and onto the slope when I added wickedly, "And the kids like you."

"I just want her for a couple of hours." Jorey sounded ill. "Do you see them?"

"There!" Pink and yellow flashed at the edge of the trees. Cement Chute didn't have curves; that's why the avalanches rolled down it so well. The colors were across the slope and a good way downhill. It could have been one wild ride for them.

The colors turned out to be the kids, huddled at the side of the slope. They'd both flopped on their butts and were gazing unhappily downhill. Jorey and I pulled up beside them with rooster tails of snow. "Steeper than you thought, huh?" They swiveled at the sound of my voice and Gracie began to cry. Todd held his arms up to me and his lower lip trembled.

"Mark!" was his one coherent word and then he howled, too. "J-j-j-j-orey!"

"Who's hurt?" I thought the kids were more scared than hurt, but I'd find out anyway. They shook their heads, but I did an assessment, kneeling in the snow, checking limbs and asking soft questions. Jorey stood over me, leaning on a pole, watching. The kids stopped crying after a bit.

"Good. Nobody's hurt." I got up and pulled them to their

feet, making sure their skis were aimed so they didn't slide. "Want to tell me what happened?"

No, they didn't want to tell me, but Gracie sniffed out, "Cal and Pete said we should, if we wanted and thought we could. They have adventures like that all the time."

"Adventures like in the movies?" The kids didn't have stunt doubles.

"Yeah." They spoke in unison.

Great, they had no awareness of fantasy vs. reality, although I wasn't a shining example of an aware adult. Cal and Pete were assholes.

"Movie adventures are made up and don't happen exactly how the story says. Skiing is just real. We'll talk about that later, okay?" I took inventory of the slope and my companions. "How are we going to get down the hill? If we go slow, can you ski it, guys?"

Jorey made a face at the word "slow" but didn't say anything, so I didn't have to punch him. Todd shook his head, and Gracie hesitated. "Maybe."

"Jorey, can you piggyback?"

He snorted. Yeah, Jorey could do it.

If the kids didn't go for that, I could call Ben at the office and have him radio a patrol to bring a toboggan, which would take up to half an hour of keeping three of us sitting in the cold. Gracie and Todd liked the idea, though.

"Yeah, piggyback! I call Mark!" Todd held his hands up again.

Gracie slid the two feet to wrap her arms around Jorey's waist. "Jorey goes faster, don't you?"

"Not piggyback, he doesn't!" It wasn't safe to race with kids aboard, and Jorey could clean my clock anyway; being an expert skier wasn't the same as being a racer. I still got a matched "Aw!"

from all three of them. "No racing, we just mosey down the hill."

"I mosey pretty fast, Gracie," Jorey assured the little girl now clinging to his back.

"Pace me," I warned him once Todd had his arms around my neck and his legs around my waist, skis waving above the snow.

I used to love Cement Chute, the fast ride down the couloir where the West Peak met the next mountain, but not anymore. Not since I'd brought Ulf's body down had I run this slope, and Ben had been understanding, not requiring me or Marty to patrol it. Now, Jorey and I wove our way downhill with children who went from hiding their faces in our necks to watching, to laughing, and calling out directions and encouragement.

"Faster, Mark!" Gracie shrieked, since Jorey was keeping just behind me.

"Faster, Mark!" Jorey agreed, laughing. I couldn't flip him off effectively with the kids on our backs.

"This is fast enough, Mark," Todd whispered in my ear, and I agreed, though I would have put on a burst of speed to get past the spot where we'd found Ulf. When we reached the curve where the slope lost much of its steepness, I stopped. Jorey pulled up beside me.

"Think you can ski it from here, kids?"

"Oh, yeah, sure we can!"

"Race you, Jorey!"

"Come on, Mark!" They wiggled down to the snow, ready to cope with this kind of terrain.

I let them start off without me, wanting to take one more moment with the slope that had screwed my life so thoroughly. Looking uphill, I shook my head at the good fortune of this day, where the mountain stayed still and quiet and everyone who skied onto that slope had skied off it again. I said a very quiet thanks to Whoever might be listening and added, "Rest in peace, Ulf." Then I turned my back on Cement Chute and hurried to catch up with the living.

Melanie waited at the junction with Killy's Knees, her face alight. The twins skied to her arms, talking over each other in the rush to tell of their adventure. Jorey watched this tender reunion with a sideways pull of his mouth, and finally told them a general goodbye that went nearly unnoticed before he left. I wanted to leave, too, but the patroller in me had to finish up the incident.

"Do we need to put a flag on your tickets so you can't ride the Upper Scott lift again, Todd? Gracie? Or do you think you can do Killy's Knees without wandering to the black diamonds?" Just give me a black marker and they could only get into trouble on the East Peak.

"We're sorry, Mark. We won't do that again," Gracie promised.

Todd nodded hard enough to rattle his brains. "That's scarier than we thought."

"It won't be, with a little more experience, but you have to have your dad's permission, and he'll tell us patrols when it's okay. The first time it's okay, I bet he'll want to go with you himself." James Underwood could ski every slope of his mountain, and what dad wouldn't want to share that?

I left them, Melanie now scolding for the fright after the joy of the safe return wore off a bit. Poor kids. But hey! *Not* "poor patroller"! I wasn't on duty, this wasn't an official incident, and there wasn't one scrap of paperwork to fill out.

TWENTY-TWO

You can't see the forest for the trees, sometimes, and I hadn't seen the mountain for the ski slopes. From the top of the West Peak, I looked around and remembered what I loved about being here. From the brilliant blue sky, striped with a few mackerel clouds and a single jet trail, the sun beat down, tanning the unwary into raccoons and lighting ranges of mountains that stretched farther than the eye could see—and I could see halfway to New Mexico. Closer, two peaks of ski runs had been groomed to perfection, calling me to their adventures. I stood at the top, admiring the irregular white paths through the trees, green close up but shading to black in the distance. Every one of those trails had quirks and delights; I knew them all and greeted them as friends. The moving figures marking the white were not my problem today, though I wished them the joy of the runs.

Which run for me? Hotdog Bun? No, I didn't want to run into Jorey again to endure his razzing. Say Your Prayers? No, I didn't want to end on the East Peak. Cement Chute? Gotta be kidding me. Killy's Knees? Not enough challenge. I was ready to stretch myself to the limit. Dynamite Alley it was.

Standing at the head of the trail, I shook out my muscles, pulled in great gouts of the cold, thin air, chose my path. And then I launched. Skating to pick up speed, I let the mountain pull me down, over snow that crackled with my passage. Weaving slightly to the left, I caught a slight rise that put me airborne, touching back to earth too soon, but still flying over the snow. Wind whistled around my sunglasses, touched my cheeks with its chill kiss, not able to hold me back. I whipped through two turns, reveling in the speed, and left the few other skiers far behind. They were only obstacles to give a wide berth, not people sharing my mountain. I crouched into a tuck at the final turn, shooting toward the lifts, feeling the blood singing through my veins.

A run like that was worth the wait in the lift line for the chance to do it again. And again. Even the rides up the mountain had their pleasures. Instead of scanning the skiers for trouble, I could puzzle out the small stories told by deer, fox, and rabbit tracks in the ungroomed snow between the trees.

I encountered the asshole actors before I called it quits for the afternoon. They were a ways ahead of me on the Lower Scott lift line; catching up with them at the top was a snap. They'd passed a flask a few times on the chairlift, so it wasn't much surprise that they fetched up in the deep powder snow at the side of Sugar Gulch, an intermediate slope that Gracie and Todd loved.

Last time I found them ass over teakettle in the snow, I pulled them out. This time, I stopped out of reach and gave them the same look I'd give the wiggling things found under rocks.

"Come on, man, give us a hand!" Cal implored, but I just

watched them struggle, thinking of children goaded into terrain beyond their abilities and men used like rental skis. I couldn't remember why I'd felt honored to be chosen for a night.

"Same kind of hand you gave those kids you encouraged to go down a black diamond?" That got cussing and glowers. They could work it out for themselves. I left.

The euphoria of a day to myself on the best snow in Colorado wore off a little once I buzzed through the shower and into the kitchen. The ever-changing cast of dinner companions would certainly include Allan, and I wanted to get him alone to patch up whatever we could patch up. The clean, cold wind in my face had lifted the miasma in my mind, giving me hope for my legal issues and for my love life. A flawless rescue and running the black diamonds and double diamonds reminded me that I was really good at what I did.

So was Allan.

And maybe he'd forgive me.

Twenty-four hours without him was too damned long, though I could see his point about ninety-six solid hours with me also being too damned long. I wanted my life back, so we could find out about normal. I wanted to hold him and tell him he was right.

None of that happened, though dinner was a far more cheerful affair than last night, as we compared notes of our days. Kurt and Jake had spent part of the day in Phippsburg, leading to a lot of speculation about what would happen to Rudi and his crew.

"Maybe nothing," Jake concluded, "if everyone but Kurt swears it was all skiing and maybe a nice lunch at the top of the mountain."

"And I don't want to do any swearing about it at all. I just want to be well away from that cretin." Kurt took a couple of bowls to the kitchen. He got out of the space next to the chair where Allan sat, and I scooted into it. I think he and Jake had stationed themselves on either side of me to head off any more hovering, but I maintained and didn't do more than hand his fork back when Allan nearly dropped it into my lap. It did make us smile at each other, though, and maybe he was remembering the fork that stuck my cheek after our first dinner together.

"That smells so good!" Gabe came in while we were still eating, a laptop under his arm. "There better be something left. I've been working my fingers to the bone, but I think this thing is operational now." He set the opened computer on the easy chair's arm and accepted the bowl Julie had filled for him. "Here, take a look." Between bites he tapped the keyboard, pointing out features.

"You could eat first, really." Allan took over the typing and I removed his empty dish, figuring this wasn't hovering, this was computer safety. Allan didn't seem to notice and nobody scolded me; they were all too busy crowding around the easy chair.

"Yeah, well, I just got this done and it works, so I'm jazzed." Gabe started inhaling a bowl of good goulash, explaining between bites. Bet he didn't even really enjoy it. "So, the incoming client starts here, adds contact info, picks days and menus from these drop-down lists, which you build from these screens over here that only you as admin can see...." I watched Allan's face as Gabe gave him a tour through his new domain. Amazement and relief, then exultation. Allan had almost looked like that when I presented him with crutches and a list of kitchen staff.

Gabe wiped his mouth with the back of his hand and went back to the computer. "Wow, that was good! Now, if you put the recipe in on this screen, it imports the numbers for the day range you pick and builds a shopping list. I thought it would help with purchasing." He lifted an eyebrow at Allan, who hadn't said he needed that function when he made his wish list.

"Oh, yes, it certainly will. Great!" Allan typed something in and smiled at the result on the screen. "And the delivery tickets I print from here…." He poked the keyboard again to a buzz of commentary from the gang about this button and that one. I watched from the side.

"Yeah. Um, I hope you still use the same credit card system you had when you started on this thing, because that's the billing I built in." For the first time, Gabe looked less than confident about what he'd created.

"Yes, I do. Oh, man, this is going to rock. Where do I get to the consolidated billing?" Allan clicked more.

Gabe looked relieved. "Right here, and you can import this into the bookkeeping software. I made it compatible with the program I found on the computer. That okay?"

"Perfect. Now what about…." They pored over the laptop, and I got up to clean the kitchen, able to contribute nothing to the electronic miracle that Allan sounded quite sure would remake his business. I couldn't help with what he needed now, and he didn't need what I could help him with, except the local version of dish pit. The running water drowned out the talk from the living room, and it drowned out my ringtone, too, but the phone vibrated in my pocket.

———

"You two are awfully quiet." James Underwood observed his youngest offspring over the dinner table. "Your appetites are fine, but where's the chatter?"

"Just, we don't want to talk today." Gracie laid her fork on her clean plate.

"Didn't you have a good time skiing with Mommy? No complaints that she went too slow?" Underwood placed a hand on his daughter's forehead. "Are you feeling okay? You haven't asked once about skiing the black diamonds."

"We can wait 'til we're six, Daddy." Gracie was uncharacteristically subdued.

"Maybe six and a half." Todd spoke to his plate.

Alarm bells jangled. "What happened to change your minds?" He kept his voice even. Melanie brought the children back without mentioning anything unusual.

The twins looked down at their plates, then at each other—anywhere but at him. Finally, they exchanged a look and Todd nodded subtly. "We tried Cement Chute, but it was too scary. Mark and Jorey came and got us," Gracie finally admitted.

"How did they know to do that?" Underwood asked the universe more than he asked the kids, his anger rising that they had been allowed on such an advanced course against his explicit orders.

"Mommy rode the lift with Jorey, so he probably saw us," Todd mumbled.

Oh, she did, did she? "Ah. And Mark, you mean tall Mark, the ski patrol with brown hair?" Underwood groped for a description.

"And the big mouth, except he wasn't wearing his patrol jacket. I didn't even know he had a blue jacket, Daddy." Gracie looked up through her lashes, but Underwood didn't take the bait of a fresh subject. Instead, he asked more questions that the kids hesitated before answering, and then sent them toward the tub with the nanny.

The computer in the office accessed everything in the

Wapiti Creek system, including patrol reports. Underwood perused the current day, finding nothing that mentioned his children. Then he pulled up the personnel folders and dialed a number.

"Yes, sir. Right. As soon as I can, sir." My caller hung up without a goodbye. I was in trouble again. I went back to the group in the living room. "How do I get to Ptarmigan Road?" The gang wrinkled their foreheads; Ptarmigan Road had only a few widely spaced mansions.

"I can give you directions, but the van's running on fumes." Allan hadn't touched me in any way tonight. Who could say the real state of the gas tank?

Jake held out some keys. "What's on Ptarmigan Road?"

"An angry James Underwood."

"What's his problem with you?" or some variation, came out of everyone.

"Jorey and I took Todd and Gracie down Cement Chute."

"What!" was the unanimous shriek, loudest from Kurt, because he was their instructor. "Why?"

"That's what Mr. Underwood wants to know. It wasn't our idea, let me tell you." I accepted the keys and turned to the pile of coats by the door where I grabbed the burgundy patrol jacket from its usual spot at the bottom of the stack.

"Uh, Mark...." Devon stopped me. Right, I'd just grabbed his pride and joy.

"Oops." I dropped it on top of the pile and dug out the blue jacket I hadn't worn much until recently. If this interview went as badly as I feared, I might never wear a burgundy jacket again.

"Come in, Mark." Mr. Underwood ushered me into a comfortable living room with a fire blazing in the massive hearth. Though he presented a businesslike façade, he had to be seething. It was no secret how he felt about his kids. "Tell me what happened today on Cement Chute."

That damned run. Every bit of crap that fell into my life came back to Cement Chute. "I noticed the kids rode the lift ahead of Mrs. Underwood, and then at the top, I saw her but not them, and started asking questions...." I told him the details, including that the kids seemed frightened into better sense but that I'd suggested restricting their lift tickets.

"You piggybacked them down. There wasn't a report." Mr. Underwood had grimaced during parts of the story, and I figured there were a few other people who would be explaining themselves before the night was out. He was certainly angry but thankfully, it wasn't aimed at me.

"I wasn't patrolling, sir, just skiing. I'm not exactly a patrol this week." I tried to meet his eyes steadily.

"Gracie mentioned a blue jacket. What happened?" He drummed his fingers on his thigh.

"I had some words with another skier, who complained. It was Mrs. Underwood, actually." Might as well tell him the whole ugly story. "Now I'm suspended for a week with no pay." Looking back, I probably had earned it, but that wasn't going to get the rent paid.

"What kind of words, Mark?" His stare bored into me, requiring an answer.

I'd already told most of this to the grand jury, but I didn't want to tell Mr. Underwood. No good could come of telling a man to his face that I knew his wife had been cheating on him.

"If it has to do with Ulf, take it as given that I know she was sleeping with him." He rubbed his eyes with one hand and then looked to me again for details.

At least I didn't have to be the one to break that particular bad news. "She blamed me for his death, because of the avalanche. I got mad and described him in some rather, uh, graphic terms." Oh, I didn't want to tell him the details, and he spared me.

"Probably nothing that I would disagree with, then, though keeping your temper will serve you better in the long run, young man." He picked up the phone and hit an autodial number.

"Ben, I hear we're short an experienced patrol this week. Mark McAvoy, yes." My boss was going to be delighted with me for getting the Big Boss to interrupt his evening. "I'm sure we are covered, but since this young man just keeps doing his job no matter what, put him back on the payroll." Mr. Underwood paused.

"I am aware of that. He won't be opening his mouth again to the skiers, I assure you." Mr. Underwood glared at me, and I didn't know whether to nod *yes, I understand* or shake *no, it will never happen again*, so I froze, which seemed to be the acknowledgment he was looking for.

"Let Devon stay on for the week, but this is how I want it, Ben. Right, consider them comp days. Except Mark will be in tomorrow to write an incident report." I nodded my understanding. It would be a very detailed report.

He hung up the call and asked another question I didn't want to answer. "Who else knows about your little spat with Melanie besides Ben?"

I looked into the fire rather than at his face. "Mr. Calhoun and the grand jury. The judge and the other court people. I'm sorry." I really was. Spreading the news of his wife's betrayal wasn't something I wanted to do, and to tell him I'd done it....

"The grand jury," he repeated. "I presume they are looking into the notion of Ulf and foul play?" He rose and poured from a decanter into a pair of cut crystal snifters that sparkled in the firelight. He handed me one; the sip from the golden puddle inside spread its fire through me. I'd never had really good brandy before.

"They are. They questioned me about how it could have happened—did anyone set it up to happen." I took another sip. A little went a long way.

"Anyone, no doubt, being me." Mr. Underwood took his own sip. "Funny, I would have bankrupted him, deported him, or worse, given him what he thought he wanted, but not killed him."

That list of possible revenges chilled me. I did not want this man angry with me. No sir, I did not. The next taste of liquid fire only partially warmed the fear away. "It never occurred to me that you did, sir. Too many things were either random or planned too far in advance. It would have been... sloppy. Uncertain."

His laugh was without mirth. "I don't use sloppy methods. Simon Calhoun has reason to know that. Someone must have made a case for it."

The brandy suddenly went down several pipes at once; I spluttered, choked, and set the snifter down rather harder than I should have. Once my internal commotion subsided, the real trouble began.

"Explain." One word to start a conflagration, and it gave me no choice.

"The whole reason I lost my temper with Mrs. Underwood

was that she suggested I set the avalanche on your direction, and then she implied you might have manipulated me into it."

"Very interesting." Mr. Underwood flicked a finger against his own snifter, getting an answering ping. "Tell me the rest."

I considered another sip of brandy, but left the Dutch courage on the table. What I'd already inhaled should ooze into my bloodstream for quite a while. I coughed again. "She knew about the subpoenas before anyone else did."

"Oh, she did? Fascinating." He swirled the brandy around the glass. "I do believe I should have a little chat with Mr. Calhoun and another with Miss Melanie. Well, Mark, I'm very sorry you've been dragged into the wreckage of my marriage."

"It happens." I'd left a whole roomful of people at home who'd been dragged into my love life one way or another. What happened between Allan and me would affect all my friends now, thanks to the way I'd made sure that everyone got to know him, and hopefully to like him. If we couldn't patch things up, would they have to choose between us? "I've got one of these situations of my own, but the stakes aren't as high as the whole resort."

"Oh?"

"Mrs. Underwood thinks she's going to end up with Wapiti Creek." I looked at the fire rather than his face.

He snorted. "That would be a case of getting what she wants, and it turns out to be a punishment. However, it would be very bad for Wapiti Creek. You needn't worry about it happening." He walked me to the door, sending me home with a handshake and higher hopes than I'd had in a while. My job was secure, someone with more firepower than I had was interested in the same side of the legal issues I was, and maybe, just maybe, Allan was still in the big easy chair.

Swinging past Kurt and Jake's place to return the car keys, I got a hit to all that new-found confidence.

"Keep them, Mark," Jake advised me. "You need to be at the courthouse at ten thirty. The process server dude showed up again with the news after you left." Wonderful. I started to ask him about Allan, what he'd said after I left, but stopped. I wouldn't drag Jake farther into the middle of my problems. He looked like he wanted to say something more, but didn't, and closed the door behind me.

At the top of the stairs, I debated turning left to 345 and knocking on Allan's door, or going right to my place, where I hoped he'd still be. If he wasn't there, I'd have a better idea of what his hopes for us were. He might be really, really tired of me. Hadn't I warned him, laughingly, that he could throw me out early if I drove him crazy?

Looked like exactly what he'd done, too. No Allan in the easy chair, no Allan waiting in my bed.

I dreamed that night, but it was the memory of Allan's body against mine that taunted me when I woke.

TWENTY-THREE

Fat white flakes were falling when I headed out to the parking lot. Marty said he'd meet me at the door when I called him about travel arrangements, and he was there waiting, but he wasn't alone. Allan waited with him.

My heart had been in my throat at the prospect of testifying again, but now it lodged there permanently. I didn't know what to say to him, but he was there, waiting, and he didn't say a thing, either. He just came out to the Toyota with us, waited at the passenger door until I unlocked it, and then got in. The drive to Phippsburg was very nearly silent, broken mostly by Allan's phone.

"Yes," he said, on more than one call, taking notes, "and the website is finally working now." Once or twice he looked at a message and smiled. After the last call, an order for two nights of dinners for six that left Allan pleased and me and Marty exchanging lifted eyebrows in the rearview mirror over the price tag, Allan put the phone in his pocket and mused aloud. "Definitely a silver lining to getting hurt. I've gotten my website fixed, improved the business, met some great people…." If he looked over at me with any great significance when he said that, I didn't see it. I was too busy staring at the road, which must have grown some great big potholes, because the shaking in the steering couldn't possibly have been from my white-knuckled hands.

Marty and Allan might have talked at the front door after I dropped them off and parked the Toyota, but the three of us were silent again once I rejoined them.

There was perhaps an inch of snow on the granite steps, and Allan had left his crutches behind and his brace off, opting instead for a pair of dress shoes that went with his suit. I said nothing, but stuck out my elbow ever so slightly. He took my arm to get up the steps without slipping. I'd offered no more help than he'd accept, and he accepted without protest. At the top, he let go, but the warmth of his hand on my arm remained.

"Gentlemen, please have a seat here in the lobby." The bailiff waved at a row of seats to one side after taking our names. I wondered who had the waiting room where we sweated out the last testimony.

A few people bustled through the lobby, some going into the courtroom through the door to our right, but then all was quiet again, and we didn't speak under the bailiff's watchful eye. Movement attracted my eye: James Underwood came into the lobby, looked around, and then opted to take a seat beside us. The fine wool coat folded over his arm spread out over his lap and into mine when he sat.

"Hello, Mark, Marty. Hello, Allan. I didn't realize you all knew one another."

We mumbled greetings. He didn't need explanations. "Are you here to testify, too?" Marty asked.

"No, I just need a few minutes' conversation with the DA." Mr. Underwood quirked one side of his mouth upward. "I imagine I can catch him in between your sessions."

There was *really* nothing to say to that. "The goulash last night was particularly good, Allan. Your Hungarian dishes always make good eating." Mr. Underwood looked satisfied with the memory of the meal.

"Thanks. My *ima*—my grandmother's recipes do go over well. She taught me to cook." Allan glanced sideways at me, and I perked up, listening for crumbs of his life. There might be a quiz later. "Though I won't put the *vesepörkölt* on the menu again. Only one order for that, from a European family. It was a disaster."

"A pity. I haven't had that since a trip to Austria." Mr. Underwood looked around at the sound of footsteps.

I would have asked what that was, except I didn't think the whole word would come out. It irritated me that Mr. Underwood and Allan shared something I didn't even understand, even if it was just a food. Then again, Mr. Underwood was treating Allan like a functioning adult, something I'd been remarkably bad at these last few days. Well, I'd get a grip, and if Allan ever offered me some of this *vese*-stuff, I'd eat it.

A woman came around the corner, dressed in a suit and holding her coat over her arm. She had short, sleek brown hair with a sprinkle of white at the temple, a bit of texture to her skin, and posture that would put a soldier to shame. She stopped in the middle of the lobby to look around, and her chin came up when she spotted us.

"Claire and I were there for—"

"James?"

Mr. Underwood was on his feet and by her side in a blur of fine wool.

"Claire!" Of all the people who might walk through the courthouse, his wife, no, his ex-wife was the last one he'd expected. Underwood squeezed the hand Claire extended. "What brings you here?"

"Oh, I thought I might find you here if I looked." He'd heard those clear tones every day for more than twenty years, but hadn't heard that much warmth directed at him in roughly eight years.

"And how did you know to even look?" Underwood would put nothing past his ex-wife; Claire had been one step ahead of most of the world for as long as he'd known her. He hadn't even managed to surprise her greatly when he got involved with Melanie. What a fool he'd been to think that a less complicated young beauty would be restful in comparison.

Claire smiled enigmatically. "Very simple."

"Charlie, right?" Underwood hazarded a guess.

"Of course. Knowing you as I do, James, I'm assuming this —ah—this—" Claire waved her hand to take in the entire courthouse and all matters there that could be laid at his door. "This is an issue without foundation?"

Underwood had no trouble looking her in the eye. "Precisely."

"Annoying all the same. What shall we do about it?" Claire had used that same phrase when told they could not purchase a parcel of land they wanted up at White Peaks. That same land was now under her control, with a ninety-nine year lease that they had negotiated originally for Underwood Enterprises, but that had been part of her divorce settlement. If Melanie gaining control of Wapiti Creek would have been very bad for the

resort, Claire's stewardship of White Peaks had been the opposite; the resort prospered in her care.

"'We'? Claire, not that I don't appreciate your help, but—"
Underwood swallowed. No, he had not properly appreciated
her help before, or there would be no Melanie coming around
the corner now. "I do think the truth is coming out, and that
will be adequate."

"If you think so, James." Claire appeared to consider. "The
truth does have a way of coming out, doesn't it?"

Underwood was suddenly very glad not to be Melanie, who
had been all but impaled on Claire's sharp glance. His second
wife stopped in her designer-shod tracks, somehow looking
tawdry and cheap compared to his confident and elegant ex.
Guilt and shock flashed across Melanie's face, and were quickly
erased, but her surety was shaken and her last few steps were
much slower than before. With some revulsion, Underwood
watched her approach and remained out of reach when Melanie
tried to take his arm.

"Oh, James, I've been so worried about you." Her voice
quavered. His would quaver, too, if Claire looked at him the
way she was looking at Melanie. Perhaps he should separate
them; this could be the meeting of the steamroller and the
creampuff. Or he could step back and enjoy the splat.

"I appreciate the concern. What brings you down here?" He
left all the sarcastic things unsaid.

"I know we aren't on the best of terms right now, but I
wanted to be here for you, to be supportive. Dear." Melanie
clutched her stylish purse, the sort that cost its weight in twen-
ties, before her chest in both well-manicured little paws. Underwood knew where those hands had been and refused to be
taken in.

"How unusual, since I'm here on business of my own, rather than business of the county." Underwood reflected that one only needed to pay proper attention to know when the woman was up to something, and regretted not having paid enough attention before. "Is something about to happen?" Claire betrayed not a thing, which he found frightening in itself.

"No, well—I don't know. Oh, James, please don't be angry with me!" She made innocent eyes at him, which he had once found delightful. "I've had to give some testimony. I do hope it won't make things difficult."

No, she was probably hoping for downright untenable.

"Stay with the truth and it should all be fine." He wondered if she even recognized the truth these days, or only what she wanted. "Oh, and Melanie, the twins really aren't ready for Cement Chute yet." He hadn't trusted himself to call her last night after the patrol's visit; it was all he could do now to sound calm. "Greens and blues when you take them out." *Nothing you can't ski yourself,* he told her yesterday when she picked them up at the house. Of course, she hadn't given them permission, she'd just been chatting with broad shoulders and couple million bucks a year in endorsements, which probably made up for the lack of an intriguing accent.

"Oh," she said faintly. "Of course."

"Lovely run, Cement Chute," Claire observed. "Nearly straight down, though, and I like a bit more curve, like Dynamite Alley. If you like that one, we'll do Gold Rush together when you come up to White Peaks." She was the voice of perfect cordiality, and yet Underwood could nearly see the flash of the twisting knife. Melanie could only emit small noises that might have been meant to be thanks.

"How convenient for me to find you all here." The court-room door had been opening and closing in the background, but now the District Attorney came through it straight to Underwood and his disparate bits of family. "Hello, James, Mrs. Underwood. Hello, Melanie." He checked his watch and glanced back at the young men. "Right on time. This part we can probably take care of without any formalities, since I really do know you by sight, but still, you know how the form must be preserved. This will take just a moment." Calhoun marched back to the cluster of young men Underwood had been sitting with, conferred with them briefly, and returned.

"Back to you, folks. Mr. Underwood, I'd surely like to have a chat with you, but I'm in the middle of something rather pressing. Could I give you a call later today, and we'll set up a meeting? It may be that certain points you'd like to discuss have been clarified by then." Calhoun spoke welcome words.

"That will be fine." Underwood handed the DA a business card. "I did have a few questions that might be better directed toward the Bureau of Land Management, regarding trespass on federal property, but I wanted your opinion, and also a question or two on libel, or perhaps it's slander." He watched Melanie out of the corner of his eye. "I might have gotten the term wrong. Maybe the word I'm looking for is perjury." He made sure to use every word Melanie would recognize as 'trouble'. She might not be clear on the distinctions, though her stricken expression suggested that one or more of those terms might apply in a personal way.

"Thank you, sir. We can certainly discuss it." Calhoun turned to Claire. "Mrs. Underwood, would you be free for lunch?" If Calhoun had had a hat to tip, Underwood would have choked him with it. Damn the man!

"Not today, Simon. Melanie and I have a lunch date." Claire spoke with such assurance that Underwood would have sworn that Melanie had really agreed to it, if Melanie hadn't been turning so very pale. "We have so much to talk about, don't we, dear? I reserved a table at the Antlers; they do a nice trout bisque."

"That they do," Calhoun agreed, turning at the sound of footsteps. "Yes, Irvin, what is it?" He took the slip of paper the silent young clerk handed him. "That was fast. Did they even leave the room?"

"No, they didn't. Fastest decision I've ever seen." The clerk raised his eyebrows briefly and left.

"Looks like some of my pressing business has been wrapped up—just had a grand jury decide 'no true bill', which happens, but now I'm thinking the county's resources have been squandered just a bit, and that irritates me." Underwood knew exactly how Calhoun felt about waste; their differing views on what constituted waste had led to most of their battles over the years. Now another Underwood, however temporary the title, was going to find out Calhoun's opinions on waste, because his attention had turned to Melanie.

"Mrs. Underwood, I'm going to have to borrow your lunch companion for a while." Calhoun glanced apologetically at Claire, who smiled sweetly.

"Not a problem. You two take care of business." Claire made a little shooing motion. "I'll wait."

Oh, indeed she would. Underwood recognized the steel that had made Claire the wife and business partner she had been. Right now, he planned to be far, far away from the Antlers, because Claire was going to have both trout bisque and Melanie for lunch.

"Do you have dinner plans, Claire?" Underwood tried to tell himself that he just wanted to find out what transpired between the two women, but knew in his heart he wanted to look at Claire over a dinner table with something to celebrate. "No true bill" was a dodged bullet, worthy of a fete. Not to mention, it would keep that bastard Calhoun at bay.

"I suppose I can delay getting back to White Peaks." Claire appeared to consider any urgent matters that might await her there. "What did you have in mind?"

"Come to the house. I can promise you something special. And no," he hastened to assure her, "Melanie won't be joining us."

"Fine, I'll see you presently." With a brief press of his hand, she dismissed him and strode across the granite floor to the seats where the young men had been.

No! Underwood needed a word with the chef—he couldn't be gone so fast! There—Allan and his companions were nearly out the courthouse door. He seldom hurried for any man, nor called out, but spoke before they reached the bottom of the outside stairs.

"Allan, a word with you." Good, he turned around and waited for Underwood to descend. "Is it too late to change or add to the dinner order for tonight?"

"Anything this late is usually 'chef's fancy', but what did you have in mind?" Allan looked prepared to be accommodating.

"Could the chef fancy chicken paprikash for four?" Underwood's memory replayed the taste of the last serving. "The kids like it, too."

"Certainly. Chicken paprikash coming up later today." Allan tapped a note into his phone.

Underwood sent them on their way with a friendly nod. "Good. There's someone I want to impress."

"Mr. McAvoy, would you recognize Melanie Underwood in business clothes?" Simon Calhoun had joined the power group there in the lobby and now came over to us. The three of us rose to greet him.

"Yes, she's standing there in the blue suit and heels." The distinguished older woman wore gray pinstripes. I wondered who she was, but Mr. Underwood was certainly more pleased to see her than he was to see his wife.

"Are you quite certain that this is the same woman who spoke to you on the chairlift?" I didn't think the DA would be asking this sort of question out in the lobby, but I wasn't going to argue.

"Totally certain. I've met her several times."

"And you, Mr. Tanquist? Is this the woman who spoke with you on the chairlift as well?"

"She is, and I'm absolutely sure." Marty's eyes narrowed, glaring past the DA at the woman in profile.

"Thank you, gentlemen. I appreciate your help, and won't take up more of your day."

We gaped at one another; all this for a certain identification? "If you care to linger, you might find out what the grand jury decides. We aren't calling any more witnesses, though I can't promise how long they'll take." Calhoun glanced at his watch, and then left us.

"That was relatively painless," Marty observed. "Do you want to go or stick around for a while?"

"We could give it a half hour," I suggested, and Allan

agreed, though it was less than ten minutes before the clerk came out to speak with the DA and then swung past us. "No true bill," he said, and Marty translated it for us with his big grin.

"The grand jury decided there's no evidence, or not enough evidence, of a crime, so no one gets charged with anything. He's off the hook, we're off the hook." At my questioning look, he qualified, "Yes, Mark, in Colorado, just like Montana and everywhere else."

"Great! Let's get out of here!" I was ready to run, but matched Allan's pace, because I was not going to hasten him into reinjuring himself. It wasn't the same as hovering. We were halfway down the steps when Mr. Underwood hailed us with his dinner request. He asked for seduction food, as I thought of it, and I could practically taste the meal that had started Allan and me on the last week's wild ride. I wished him better luck with his plans than I'd had.

"Are you all headed back to the same place, or does anyone need a lift back to Wapiti Creek?" Mr. Underwood asked. I understood his expansive mood, because weren't he, Marty, and I all released from suspicion?

"I'll ride with you, if I may." Marty was so fast to answer that he might have accepted a lift to Denver as a good way to avoid the discomfort of another silent trip with us. With me. It was being around me that was everyone's problem.

The drive wasn't silent on the way back.

"You said Mr. Underwood was angry last night, but he was fine just now. What happened?"

"He's probably seen the incident report I filed this morning." I'd been up as early as any work day to get that paperwork finished, and Ben had only razzed me a little about getting back into the Big Boss's good graces the dramatic way. "He wasn't angry with me. I wasn't the one who let the kids get away."

The details of that got us most of the way back to Wapiti Creek, behind a big silver SUV that Marty was no doubt finding much more comfortable than the backseat of the crudmobile.

"So, another couple days of vacation and then back as usual?" Allan summed it up. "And no one's accusing you of any crime, so no more worries there."

Words weren't adequate for the relief on that last, and having a paycheck again was its own solace. "And my apartment's clean, the sheets are fresh, and I've been eating better lately. In fact," I paused to park the Toyota before continuing, "everything in my life is damned near roses." Except my love life, and he'd told me to back off. I was staying backed.

"Mine's not."

I whipped my head around at that soft comment.

"Well, most of it. But the part that sucks is that I slept alone last night." He looked at my face, then away. "Mark, are you always this 'all or nothing'?"

"Isn't that one of the things you have to hang around me to find out?" Some bitterness made me return his words to him, and then I regretted them. "No, not usually, I think."

"Maybe that is one of the things I do have to stick around for." Allan tried prying my fingers off the gearshift knob, which was probably going to sport some dents now. When I realized it, I made a conscious effort to relax, letting him take my hand in his. "Mark, I missed you."

"I was hoping you'd gone to sleep in my bed last night." My grip strengthened before I knew it, though his grip was just as strong, holding me tightly but not letting me crush him.

"Not without talking to you. Or everything that's a problem

would just keep being a problem." He raised my knuckles to his lips for a soft velvet stroke. "I hoped you'd knock on my door."

"I thought about it. I thought you'd still be at my place, if that's where you wanted to be at all." The console and gearshift lay between us. I could probably hug him over the knobby bits, at the risk of hurting him.

"That's where I'd like to be now."

TWENTY-FOUR

"You don't have to be in the kitchen?" I asked on our way in. Call me a fool for looking a gift horse in the mouth, but he'd already used a chunk of his day that he usually spent cooking.

"No. Got everything simmering. I had two extra sets of hands helping this morning, since it was pretty unanimous that I should be with you." Allan stepped around an icy patch on the parking lot. "We got it all done early."

"Kim's been meddling again." She'd really gotten this entire relationship rolling, but I couldn't blame her if I'd let it roll right off a cliff.

"Not just Kim. I got the law laid down to me last night, after you left." We started up the stairs, but by the last flight, Allan was visibly struggling, even with one hand on the railing. I stuck my elbow out at him again, and we got him the rest of the way to the third floor. "Guess I need to put on the brace for more walking. Anyway, they strongly suggested that I either fix things or break it off cleanly with you."

"Did 'strongly suggested' include death threats?" I knew my friends.

"Not sure. Do you think I'd survive getting my guts used for climbing ropes?" He watched me unlock the door, then followed me into my apartment.

"Was that Kim, Kurt, or Jake?" They all rock-climbed, though it sounded more like Kim's sort of threat.

"Julie, actually. Quite a bloodthirsty mind under all that hair—I was surprised." Allan shed his coat on top of mine. "So was Gabe. Anyway, my point is, your friends very much want you to be happy, which is good, because I do, too." He stepped against me and put both hands behind my neck. "Mark, you can learn a lot about a man by how his friends feel about him. They really care about you."

I slipped my arms around his waist, under the suit coat. "I know. So, they frightened you into coming with me?" Damn, he smelled good, something citrus and spicy, and I had to be this close to get even a whiff. The smell made me want to put my lips against his neck and nibble.

"No, they made it possible for me to be with you without a lot of people eating thawed-out 'chef's fancy' tonight or making other dinner plans." He was so warm, so near, and looked up at me with such transparent honesty that I had to reach down for a small kiss. Just a little brush of lip against lip, letting me think about what he'd just said. "Mark, they didn't have to threaten me to make me want to get things square with you."

"How much convincing did they take?" I found his mouth again, delaying his answer.

"Once the process server showed to say you and Marty had to go back to court and I said, 'Screw the food, I'm going,' they were convinced. I think." He pulled me closer. "If they see us together and you're smiling, the lingering doubts should be gone."

"What about your lingering doubts?" I stroked one hand up

and down his back, and yes, I was trying to influence the answer.

"Those we cure with prolonged exposure to a Mark who isn't trying to cope with his whole world caving in plus a new relationship." Allan started running his fingers through my hair, brushing the long strands back from my face.

"I really was a pain in the ass." Sticking my hand into his trousers let me grip the offended body part. "I don't think it will be a problem now."

"Better not be." Okay, I hadn't exactly apologized, and he hadn't exactly accepted, but we seemed to be on the same page now, because he was flexing into my hand. "What about your lingering doubts?"

I didn't have any lingering doubts. I wanted him and I loved him, and if he still thought it was too soon, I'd just keep it to myself. "They might be totally resolved if I knew what the *vese*-stuff is."

He laughed. "You can't be serious. It's *vesepörkölt,* and it's well…." He groped for a translation. "Kidney stew is what I think I called it on the menu."

Ew! went through my head but not out my mouth. Insulting his grandmother's cooking was not the way back into his affections. "Traditional Hungarian recipe?" He nodded as though he was braced to hear the exclamation anyway. "Like Vencel is a traditional Hungarian name?"

"My grandfather's. But I'm not going to tell you the story now, because we're standing here when we could be in bed together, where we haven't been for two days." Allan nibbled along my jaw line.

My own priorities were leaning much more toward getting naked than hearing family history, too, so I rubbed my groin against him. "Better save me some stories for later." Pulling him against me using a double handful of warm round butt let me feel his answering desires; opening my mouth to his tongue made them grow.

With his arm around my waist and mine around his shoulders, we got to the bedroom without finding out if I was offering exactly the right amount of support or just an embrace.

Didn't matter; we were there and the clothes were coming off as fast as we could unbutton. Allan pushed me over to strip off my trousers, got my underwear in the same motion, and slapped my ass. "That's for being a pain. Now we start over."

Fine by me—it was like coming home to have him drop down on top of me, spread his solid warmth against my ribs. He was heavy and comforting—he was passionate and wild— he ground against my mouth and groin, taking my breath away. I couldn't touch enough of him with only two hands and a mouth; wrapping my legs around his hips was almost enough to hold him tightly. If he entered me now, it might be enough, but we hadn't greased up and he only brushed against my cheek with promises.

Allan bucked when I caught the ridge of his shoulder, letting the muscle roll as I bit him, not hard enough to break skin or bruise, but more than enough to bring a cry of pleasure. "I'm going to eat you up!" I declared wickedly, then took another bite and flicked my tongue mercilessly against the captured flesh.

"You do that," he mumbled, thrusting against my groin and catching my earlobe for a good long sucking of its own. But he must have decided he'd eat me up instead, because he started a nibbling, licking path down my body, stopping here and there to mouth me more thoroughly, which interrupted the xylophone tune his tongue played down my ribs. He licked the line of my ribcage and found every ridge in my abs before moving lower to dart his tongue into my navel. I couldn't help bouncing from the tickle, which poked the end of my cock into his chin.

He took the hint.

The wet heat of his mouth undid me. I wanted to thrust madly against that firm tongue and down his throat, but he placed both hands on my hips and pinned me to the bed. Using his strength, his weight, and finally a sexy glance to still me, he took total control of what we were doing, and I could only lie back and be pleasured. The thousand different caresses Allan danced over the head and shaft trailed down into my balls and once into a rather firm lick across my thigh.

"Spread for me, Mark," he coaxed, and then his fingers found my crack while he tongued the soft skin behind my balls. "Yeah, oh, we are so gonna mow you." He licked his own arm this time, slipped the head of my cock back into his mouth, then hastily licked his own arm again. "Where's the lube?" He spread my cheeks wide with thumb and forefinger, letting the air tease me while he groped in the bedside table. "Ah. More strawberry condoms."

Slippery fingers in my ass and slippery tongue in my mouth, Allan leaned against me, prepping me for what I desperately wanted. He spread his fingers, stretching me, making me twist to plaster more of my body against him. He took his time and I didn't try to hurry him, though I burned for what was coming. Choking back the begging, but maybe not the whimpers, I was more than ready to "Roll over, Mark." Glad to comply, I raised my ass, spreading my thighs to let him settle.

He splayed over me, chest to my back, his thighs against mine, and oh, his cock at my back door, pressing and then entering, pushing a small cry out of me. "You okay?" he whispered against my back. I squeezed his hands to tell him yes, better than okay, and then way better than okay with his slow strokes. "You doing good?" Yeah, but I didn't have the words so I sucked one of his fingers into my mouth and gave it everything he'd given my cock before.

Every leisurely thrust pushed him deep into my ass, rubbed my own hard cock against the ridged seams of my quilt. Meeting him at the unhurried pace he set was making me want Allan to just pound himself into me, yet I wouldn't change our rhythm. Allan was directing traffic here, driving me mad in the process. I started nipping at the pads of his hand, the chef's insulation that cushioned his touch, and he replied by lipping and licking the back of my neck.

Then his weight was off me, and his hips slammed against my ass, his cock fast and probing deep, but he changed again with a gasp. His wrist, I thought distantly, but those strong hands hauled me to my knees with less effort than it had taken to move the stockpot, dragging me back onto his shaft again and again. I could only scream wordlessly into my forearm and use the other hand to give myself the grip and friction that Allan was getting from my ass.

He froze, pulsing into me and holding his breath until he let loose with a groan that started somewhere around his navel. I was too close to stop; my own hand would have to make up for his thrusting. He held my cheeks tight against his hips. I could get there, I was nearly there, and then I came upright to press against him. Allan plastered me against his chest and took over the furious pumping. The tiny break in rhythm set me back just enough to know that it was his hand, not mine, and his arm across my chest kept me from collapsing when I came, splashing my overturned palm with semen.

Leaning against each other was probably all that kept us kneeling instead of toppling. Tilting my head back, I still couldn't rest it on his shoulder, but I could turn enough to meet his eyes, and I did have the presence of mind to flip my full hand over before it dripped empty. His lips were out of sight but the smile crinkled the corners of his eyes, and I'd have kissed him if I could have only reached.

"Meet you back here." He disengaged with a little swipe to my shoulder blade to let me stagger to the laundry basket and wipe my hand on yesterday's whiffy polypropylene long johns. When we crawled back on the bed, we got our heads on the pillow this time. We held each other, lazily kissed whatever bits of face were handy, and drowsed with happy exhaustion. Allan was warm against my skin, his hair a dark blur of short wavy brown at such close range, and his breathing was all the music I needed to hear. His citrus/spice cologne mixed with the scent of his skin and sweat and the sex. I was content, ready to stay there for hours, the afternoon, days, weeks.

Months. Years. In my mind, the empty corner of the bedroom filled with Allan's old oak dresser; maybe the mirror would tilt so we could see ourselves in bed. The half-empty closet filled with his clothes; his couch went into the living room, where it would stay folded up unless we wanted to bounce on it. Our friends would have a place to sit when they joined us for dinner; I'd have to get to know the cinnamon roll people. We'd have a table to eat on when it was just us. If the one in his kitchen now was Randi's, we'd buy one together. I nibbled the edge of his ear—it was right there, in perfect range—and kept my dreams to myself.

Allan would only tell me it was too soon.

Maybe.

"Are you sure it's not okay for me to love you just a little bit?" I whispered.

"I'm sure it's not okay." Allan left no doubt.

"I know you better now. Your shoe size is nine and a half,

your birthday is February 27, you don't like being smothered but you'll accept the help you need, your middle name is Vencel, traditions are important in your family, and, oh, I don't know about the chocolate. Which did you eat first?" Could I persuade him?

"I should not be eating any chocolate at all, but I saved it to eat with you, since it looked like an experiment. We still haven't seen each other normal. This is all relief." The kiss he brushed over my face qualified his "no."

"How much normal do we have to see?" How long before I could risk saying anything again?

"How about until I can't feel your ribs?" His hand was playing marimba up and down my chest. "Or until you're insulated enough to not need the smelly kind of long underwear?"

I had to laugh. If that was his time frame, I'd be eating thirds of his good cooking at every opportunity. "Okay."

Then Allan drove every bit of amusement out of me. "Mark, I don't really want you to love me a little bit."

"You don't?" Why didn't he just leave me instead?

"No." Allan took my chin in his hand, made me look into his eyes. "If you love me at all I want you to love me a lot."

ABOUT THE AUTHOR

P.D. Singer lives in Colorado with her slightly bemused husband, one proto-adult, and twelve pounds of cats. She's a big believer in research, firsthand if possible, so the reader can be quite certain Pam has skied down a mountain face first, been stepped on by rodeo horses, acquired a potato burn or two, and will never, ever, write a novel that includes skydiving.

When not writing, playing her fiddle, or skiing, she can be found with a book in hand.

Follow the adventures at Pam's website.

Keep current with Pam and the Rocky Ridge gang by joining the newsletter.

MORE MARK AND ALLAN

You can bet Mark's anxious to fulfill Allan's conditions. Here's a Valentine's Day short where it all comes true, plus a sweet bit of established couple fun.

Storm on the Mountain

When driving snow and high winds force the Wapiti Creek Ski Resort to shut down the lifts, ski patrol Mark wants nothing more than to round up the last stragglers and get safely indoors. Chef Allan is still out in the blizzard on a borrowed snowmobile, delivering meals so a hundred people don't go hungry. While Mark's protective instincts scream to drag his lover inside, he respects Allan's need to honor commitments, even at the risk of frostbite.

Allan's got another problem bigger than the storm. Mark has the solution -- but Allan will never accept it if they don't reach the decision together.

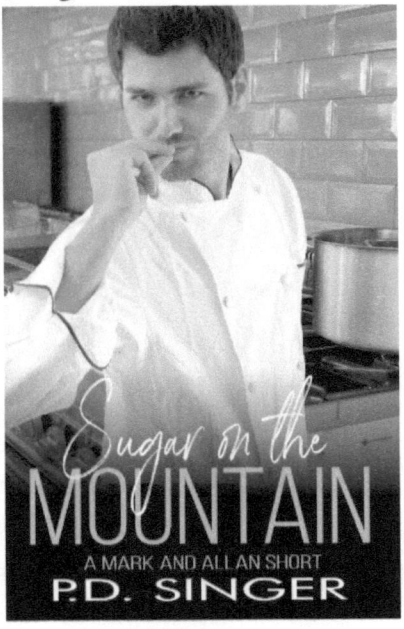

Sugar on the Mountain

Chef Allan Tengerdy becomes alarmed when his lover Mark McAvoy starts exhibiting some very odd behavior. *Please* let that twitch be an affectation, and why the hell is he calling Allan "sugar"?

ALSO BY P.D. SINGER

Fire on the Mountain

Snow on the Mountain

Blood on the Mountain

Return to the Mountain

Running to Him

Spokes

The Rare Event - returning soon

A New Man - returning soon

Diving Deep - returning soon

Concierge Service

A PREVIEW OF BLOOD ON THE MOUNTAIN

CHAPTER 1 (A JAKE AND KURT NOVEL)

I sighted down the arrow nocked against the bowstring, trying to focus on the target instead of the chill breeze blowing across my bare ass.

Quite aside from the fact that I was shivering alone, I would *not* allow Kurt to have the last laugh in this little contest. He remained admirably silent in spite of watching my attempts to aim between shudders, although I knew he was dying to bust out laughing and demand another piece of clothing as forfeit. I was running out of things to take off.

Taking advantage of a lull in the breeze, both for my comfort and for my aim, I released my arrow. It flew with a slight upward curve, slicing through the air and coming down in perfect alignment with the gold ring in the near center of the target. The *znng* of the bowstring still hissed near my ear when the arrow struck—I'd learned to hold my stance those extra seconds to avoid introducing a bad vector to my shot.

"Good one, Jake!"

Kurt Carlson, my lover, my self-appointed archery coach, and my current opponent, had spent a big chunk of last summer's ranger season chivvying me into a semblance of competence with his long bow, which was both shorter and with a heavier draw weight than I needed. This year, I was armed, literally, with a bow that suited my reach, and my prowess had increased by leaps and bounds.

Not enough to keep me dressed in our game of strip archery, though. Even with well-fitted equipment and improved skills, I was standing at the shooting line wearing nothing but socks and boots. Kurt still had his ranger-green T-shirt and utility pants on, though my one very good shot cost him his hat.

My hat, utilities, shirt, and underwear lay in a ranger-green heap near a clump of mountain mahogany. At this point, I could only hope that the sight of my near-naked body would distract Kurt into muffing his shot. So far it wasn't working—he'd seen me often enough in the last year that the novelty had to have worn off a little, although his enthusiasm for the view certainly hadn't. Maybe if I was rubbing against him, or was slightly erect, but the breeze had raised a couple of goose bumps on my back end and done that shrinkage business in front. A safety measure, really. The last thing I needed was a close encounter between my dick and the bowstring.

"Your shot." I ceded the shooting line to him, prepared to lose a sock.

He lifted his bow, arrow to the string, the late afternoon light filtering through the trees that ringed our little meadow to tip the ends of his blond hair with gold. With his back to me, his arm holding out the bow, and his face in profile, all he needed was a hunting horn to turn our Colorado mountain into Sherwood Forest. Looking at him, I knew I was lucky to have won even one round.

In spite of the stakes, we played fair; he didn't laugh at me, and I didn't cough or otherwise distract him. But should I warn him about the fly?

Not knowing if it was the biting sort, though it was big, dark, and not flying in a straight line, I held my tongue. Kurt pulled his bowstring back. I covered my groin.

It whizzed at me, veering off when I swatted at it with my free hand. Cutting past Kurt's ear, it *bzz*ed away without stopping for a taste.

But the damage was done.

Kurt danced sideways to avoid the fly at the exact moment he released the bowstring. The arrow arced up and came down near a low clump of yellow flowers, yards from the hay bales that supported our target.

"Agh!" He waved his bow to chase away the fly, and then an even louder, "*Agh!*" when he realized how badly he'd shot. "Interference."

"Natural hazard." I grinned at him. A puff of wind had stolen one of my earlier shots out of the gold ring and onto the edge of the red ring, costing me my utilities, so I wasn't exactly sympathetic.

"Where'd it go?" He scanned the meadow. The pink fletching that should have made the arrow easy to find made the arrow look like a wildflower now, though the columbines, closest in shape and color, preferred the shade of the aspens.

"I shot an arrow in the air; where it fell I knew not where," I quoted. "The bad shot will make me go bare, the arrow landed over there." Between mangling Longfellow and pointing, I earned one of Kurt's glares, his Colorado-sky-blue eyes slitted against the sun and bad rhymes. "Shirt. Off."

"I'm still ahead," he mumbled through the cotton he dragged over his head. He tossed his T-shirt at the pile of clothing.

"We both win," I pointed out reasonably. "Could be worse." I slid one hand over my chest and down to my hip, my sense of fair play succumbing to the magnificent sight of his muscular torso. If my next shot was going to be tougher because of his naked chest, I'd even up the distraction.

"More bare skin for the fly." Kurt trailed one finger over his nipple.

Okay, two could play at that game, but since I was six feet of exposed hide, less a few inches protected by my work boots, I was feeling a little more vulnerable. I shook my ass, making my equipment swing. Even with the shrinkage, there was a fair amount of me flapping. "If it comes back, I'll swat it for you."

"You'd knock it into next week." Kurt's dimple, there at the right corner of his mouth, made an appearance. "If you were hard. I could help with that."

He most certainly could, and was. Except.... "Two more shots finishes this. Three, maybe."

I had two socks yet as my stake—we'd agreed that boots were safety, not clothing, when it came to strip archery. We couldn't afford to be less than effective from something as stupid and avoidable as stepping on a sharp rock barefooted. Not when we'd have a fire to fight sooner or later, or wildlife to evade. Danger in the Uncompahgre National Forest came in more than one flavor.

"Two." He grinned at me. "If you need to take it to the bitter end."

Bastard. Okay, I have a competitive streak, not quite as wide as Kurt's, but it's still there, and I didn't plan to give up so easily. I'd make him work for it—with a little luck, I could stretch this out to four shots. I didn't have any real hope of winning, but a man has his pride.

Besides, I felt the need to test myself under pressure. Last year, when Kurt had been attacked by a biker, I'd driven the guy off by shooting him in the Harley. Since I'd been trying to skewer his big beer belly, nailing his gas tank had to be considered pure dumb luck, both for the hit and for running him off. I didn't intend to depend on luck like that ever again. Kurt was far too precious to me.

Which didn't mean that he wasn't a distraction now. I willed my mind back to driving my eyes and hands instead of my cock. Being very, very careful not to bring the bow near enough to catch on my bobbing semierection, I took position, aimed, and fired.

"Bull's-eye!" Kurt licked his lips and took his own shooting stance. I'd hit the gold center circle, but it was two inches across —he could possibly come nearer the exact middle.

Thwap!

He did, eying me archly. I balanced against him to pull my boot off. I waved my sock at him, because there had to be some upside to losing again, stuffed my bare foot back into the boot, and added his winnings to the pile of clothing. One last chance to delay defeat.

His hand was warm on my back. "We don't have to play this all the way out, Jake." He slid his hand lower, cupping my ass.

"We don't," I agreed, pulling him close and finding his mouth. Another game two could play at. I let him sink against me, and for a moment, I was tempted to just call it good right there, break off the competition, and slide my hand under the olive-green denim covering his ass. "But we're going to." I finished the kiss with a pop. "You shoot first this time."

"Not fair." He was as hard as I was, proving it by thrusting his groin against mine, and I cursed the clothing and my competitiveness. "We shoot at the same time."

Still not exactly equal: one of us would be in line of sight of the other. I'd do my best to ignore him. "Fair enough." My arrows had blue fletching; there wouldn't be any issue knowing which arrow flew truest.

He turned his back to me, selecting an arrow and settling his feet at shoulder's width apart. Kurt was only two inches shorter than I, which meant that his wide shoulders stayed in my field of vision, and if I dropped my eyes to his narrow butt, I might as well unstring my bow right then and declare him the winner.

With arrow to string, I told him, "Fire at will."

If Will had been strapped to the bull's-eye, he'd have been perfectly safe. My arrow hit the edge of the hay, but Kurt's went wild. Had the fly come back? Surely I hadn't rattled him that much with a smooch and a grope.

"You okay?"

"Yeah," Kurt told me, standing abruptly straighter with his chin upthrust. Guess I had shaken his concentration, but I had won the round, even if my shot was lousy.

"Utilities." Such was the penalty for distraction. Then I had to look away when the globes of his ass thrust out at me as he bent to pull off his boots and slide his britches off. Something heavy sagged the cargo pockets on each trouser leg. His folding knife on one side, probably, but I hadn't seen him slip anything else in. Kurt tended to go prepared for all eventualities. Better not think about that too hard.... With laces flapping, he poked his feet back into his boots, leaving his utilities in a puddle on the ground. He would have to choose today to go commando.

"One more arrow." I really didn't think I could win another round to tie it. Not when I was shooting against a man with more skill and enough aggression to make the US Ski Team, and facing his bare behind.

"One more."

If I was going to go down, I would do it in style. Regulating my breathing so my body's motions wouldn't influence my projectile, I tried to calm myself enough to shoot between heartbeats. Good luck with that, but the blue ring of the target and my arrowhead lined up, with the expectation that gravity would pull it down the few inches to the gold bull's-eye. I'd learned to aim above what I expected to hit at this range.

"Fire at will." Kurt gave the signal this time, something I heard only distantly; all my focus was thirty yards away.

Becoming the arrow was beyond me, but this might be the closest I'd ever come to Zen archery. I watched the arrows fly, with time slowed enough to see that one trailed the other slightly, pink fletching to the rear, and when they hit, they seemed to hit together. I came back to myself.

"Can you tell from here?" The fletchings looked like they touched.

"Nope." Kurt looked surprised. Well, if he was expecting to rattle me with the sight of his naked backside, I'd messed with his perceptions. I should have insisted we swap off who stood to the right.

We wouldn't be shooting again, so another kiss and cuddle before we went down range to collect our arrows wouldn't have made a difference, but Kurt strode off, collecting the arrow he'd lost to the fly's attack. He examined the yellow flowers carefully before marching on.

"Something weird about the plant?" I asked. It was low growing with grayish-green leaves, and I didn't have a name for it.

"Just checking to see if it's a native. We were told to keep an eye out for invasive species, remember?"

I did recall, but my ability to tell one gray-green plant with yellow flowers from another was pretty limited—this could be one of three species. "Is it?" I looked closely, trying to decide what the identifying characteristics were.

"Yes, it's alpine avens. I thought it might be California poppy, but the flowers are smaller and the petals shaped differently. Besides, it's kind of hard to tell what the home range for California poppy is. That's found all over the West." Kurt bent to collect his wild arrow, which had fallen short of the target by several paces. He tucked it between his fingers, careful not to foul the fletching on the arrow he already held.

"I thought poppies were red."

"The garden kind comes in all sorts of colors, but California poppies are yellow, and prickly poppies are white. Those are native around here. There's a huge stand of them by the scarp. About knee-high."

Did we have a field of morphine plants in the middle of our national forest? Nah.

We reached the target and started to remove the arrows, starting with the ones farthest from center, mostly mine. We halted on the last two projectiles, one fletched blue, one fletched pink, that straddled the line between the center gold circle and the gold ring just outside it that made the bulls-eye. Mine was a few millimeters closer to the center. I blinked, unsure of what I was seeing.

Kurt pulled back a fraction of an inch. "Pretty good shooting, Jake."

"Uh, I guess you owe me a sock." I touched the arrows again, just to be sure I'd really accomplished this feat, before pulling one out of the target. Faced with nothing but the evidence of really good shooting, no distractions or insects helping, I wasn't sure what to make of this. Besting Kurt by even this fraction just didn't match my perceptions. Staying in hailing distance, yes. Beating him, no. I lay the arrow on top of the hay, ready to pull out the evidence.

"I guess I do." He toed off a boot.

"No, don't. Not here. You'll only lose it." Not anywhere. I yanked out the second arrow. Kurt's socks led a life of their own, since he couldn't seem to hit a laundry basket with them, but I didn't want an escapee on the archery range.

"Looks like a tie." He touched the holes in the target's fabric and turned to me, his face tilted enough to reach my lips.

"No, you still won. You didn't have any underwear on." That thought steadied me a little.

"Don't worry about it, Jake. It's okay." He brushed his mouth across mine. "That last arrow should take all." He slipped his hands around my waist to pull me close—I took his shoulders and nuzzled back. "I'm declaring you the winner." Picking up where he left off earlier, he rubbed his nude body against mine.

"Kurt, what are you doing?" I asked when he dropped out of kissing range, licking a trail down my chest, my belly, to my cock, which perked up under his breath.

"Going down in defeat, Hot Stuff."

Read the rest.

ALSO FROM ROCKY RIDGE BOOKS

The Diversion Series from Eden Winters

Diversion

Collusion

Corruption

Manipulation

Redemption

Reunion

Suspicion

Decision

The Wrestling Series from D.H. Starr

Wrestling With Desire

Wrestling with Love

Wrestling With Passion

Wrestling with Hope

The Dark Angels Series from Z. Allora

With Wings

Tied Together

Finally Fallen

www.ingramcontent.com/pod-product-compliance
Lightning Source LLC
Chambersburg PA
CBHW020359210626
46816CB00006BB/2047